ONE String

ALEATHA ROMIG

NEW YORK TIMES BESTSELLING AUTHOR

A Riverbend Lighter One

An enemies-to-lovers, fake-date, little-sister's-best-friend, second-chance, forbidden, contemporary "lighter" ONE stand-alone romance

ALEATHA ROMIG

New York Times, Wall Street Journal, and USA Today bestselling author

COPYRIGHT AND LICENSE INFORMATION
ONE STRING

2024 Edition
ISBN: 978-1-956414-91-2
Editing: Silently Correcting Your Grammar
Proofreading: Stacy Zitano Inman
Cover Art: RBA Designs/ Romantic Book Affairs
Formatting: Romig Works LLC

Aleatha Romig's most recent and upcoming releases

BOUND BY A PROMISE – Brutal Vows, book three - September 2024

Arranged marriage, age-gap, forbidden, mafia/cartel stand-alone romance

ONE STRING – July 2024

Aleatha's Lighter Ones - Second-chance, enemies-to-lovers, fake-date, little-sister's-best-friend, forbidden, stand-alone contemporary romance

TILL DEATH DO US PART – Brutal Vows, book two - June 2024

Arranged marriage, enemies to lovers, Mafia/cartel stand-alone romance

NOW AND FOREVER – Brutal Vows, book one - May 2024

Arranged marriage, age-gap, mafia/cartel stand-alone romance

LIGHT DARK – April 2024

Cult, psychological thriller, forced proximity, romantic suspense stand-alone

*Previously published through Thomas and Mercer as INTO THE LIGHT and AWAY FROM THE DARK

REMEMBERING PASSION – Sinclair Duet book one – September 2023

Scorching hot, second-chance romance filled with the suspense and intrigue

REKINDLING DESIRE – Sinclair Duet, book two – October 2023

Scorching hot, second-chance romance filled with the suspense and intrigue

For a complete list of all Aleatha Romig's works, turn to BOOKS BY ALEATHA at the end of this novel.

One String

Enemies-to-lovers, fake-date, little-sister's-best-friend, second-chance, forbidden, stand-alone contemporary romance.

Ricky Dunn is the equivalent of a splinter under my fingernail.

Romantic?

Right.

He's the older brother of my best friend, and no matter how hard either of us tries, we can't seem to avoid each other. The problem started on the night my best friend and I graduated from high school. The party was joyous, a celebration.

That night, I willingly gave Ricky a part of me—more than the kiss we told others about.

Our deal was simple.

No strings.

Ricky kept his side of the bargain.

Years have passed.

Being from the same small town and crossing paths, I haven't noticed how handsome he's become or the way he's filled out.

If you ask me, he hasn't noticed me either.

Until he calls.

I'm working for a finance company, one he's now interviewing for.

"Marilyn, will you be my date for the dinner with the partners? It's only for one date and no strings."

The problem is my heart hasn't kept my side of our bargain.

I want at least one string.

Do I agree to his proposal, or do I turn him down flat?

Have you been Aleatha'd?

Check out Aleatha's 2024 Lighter One—ONE STRING—enemies-to-lovers, fake-date, little-sister's-best-friend, second-chance, forbidden, stand-alone contemporary romance.

Chapter One

Marilyn

"You look beautiful," I say to Devan, one of my best friends and my roommate during four years of college. Devan, Jill, and I have been friends since before we started kindergarten. Only two weeks ago, I was the maid of honor in Jill's wedding. And now, here we are again, the three of us getting ready to walk the aisle of the church in our hometown, Riverbend, Indiana. This time, it isn't Jill who's dressed in white; it's Devan.

She takes a deep breath and stares at her own reflection. "I'm not nervous." Her big soft-brown stare turns to me. "Shouldn't I be?"

Jill is the one to answer. With her long auburn hair pinned up in a twist, her green gaze shines. "There's nothing to be nervous about when you know the man waiting for you at the end of the aisle is the one." She rubs Devan's shoulder. "Justin is your forever. I felt the same way knowing Todd and I were meant to be." Jill turns to me. "I'm right, aren't I?"

I half chuckle. While my two best friends have found their forevers, mine is still wandering the earth, assuming he's out there at all. Instead of replying directly, I smile, meeting Devan's gaze in the reflection. "You know I was skeptical about you and Justin in the beginning, but he's proven me wrong and so have you. You two are perfect together."

Devan reaches for my hand and Jill's at the same time. "I'm so glad you're both here to share this day with me." She squeezes my hand. "Your wedding will be next."

I shake my head, feeling the dangling pearl earrings tickle my neck. "While you two live in married bliss, I'm going to take the world of finance by storm. I don't have time for a man in my life."

Devan's lips curl. "When the right one comes along, you'll make time. In the meantime, we know you'll climb the ladder of success. You're kicking ass at Parker and Stevens."

Parker and Stevens is one of the top wealth management companies in the Midwest. Their corporate office is on the north side of Indianapolis.

I was lucky enough to land an internship there. I'm hoping that after I finish my master's degree in finance, I will be able to say I'm employed by Parker and Stevens.

"Today is about you," I reply. "Are you ready to take on the last name of Sheers?"

Before she can answer, the door to the dressing room opens, and Molly, Justin's seven-year-old niece, bounds inside with her mom Kandace on her heels. Molly's voice fills the room. "Uncle Justin is wearing a tie." She tilts her head and makes a dreamy face. "He looks so handsome."

Kandace shakes her head at her daughter and speaks to Devan. "You're beautiful. Justin is a lucky guy."

A rosy hue fills Devan's cheeks. "I think I'm the lucky one."

"Are you ready?" Kandace asks. "Jack is waiting outside the door."

Devan takes a deep breath. "This is really it."

Jill and I nod and reach for our bouquets. "Love you," we say in unison to Devan.

"Love you too."

Kandace opens the door and leads Molly toward the chapel. Jill and I follow, giving Devan some time alone with her dad. Jack's eyes glisten as he nods our way.

Once we're out of earshot of Devan, Jill whispers. "Are you good?"

"I'll be an old maid for the rest of my life, but other than that, yeah, I'm great."

"I mean about Ricky."

Pressing my lips together, I inhale. "I'm fine. I'll be better when the reception is over, and we can go back to hating each other."

"You don't hate each other."

"I can play nice for Devan, but I'll be honest, I'm glad that once today is done, I won't have to see or talk to Ricky Dunn for the rest of my life."

We stop at the end of the hallway, waiting for our cue to walk down the aisle. Organ music fills the air, and Jill is waved over. She flashes me a knowing smile and begins her walk toward the front of the church. I'm next. Standing in the open doorway, I see Justin, the groom, standing with his hands clenched in front of him. Ricky and Dax Richards, Kandace's husband, are at his side.

If only Devan had asked Jill to be her maid of honor, I wouldn't be stuck walking the aisle and being paired with Justin's best man, Richard Dunn, aka Ricky. I haven't always hated the man. Since he was my best friend's older brother, there was a time I had a crush on him. I mean, I considered him handsome in a rugged way. Growing up and hanging around Devan's home, I was admittedly an admirer, even though he is ten years older than us.

The thing is that back then, Devan's brother didn't notice us, not even his sister. To him, we were all little girls. The fact that now Devan is marrying Ricky's best friend and bridging that age gap is far from my story. No, my story hasn't turned out the same.

There was one night, the night of Devan's graduation party—we had just graduated from Riverbend High School—that I bravely approached Ricky. No longer a little kid, I was an adult, and it was my intention for him to see me that way. The only person I ever told about what happened that night is Jill. No matter how great of friends Devan and I are, I couldn't tell her what I'd given Ricky that night. Jill and I swore to keep it a secret. Heaven knows, afterward, Ricky made no attempt to follow through on any kind of relationship, not even friendship.

"Marilyn," Mrs. Johnson, a woman from the church, whispers. "It's your turn."

Smiling, I nod.

I can play nice for my best friend. And once this day is over, I can wipe Ricky Dunn from my shoes for the last time. There is a giant world outside of Riverbend, and that's where I plan to live. If love comes along, great. If it doesn't, I can live with that too.

With each step upon the runner, I do my best to

keep my gaze averted from the man I will soon be partnered with. The best man and the maid of honor. Despite my best efforts, I can't help but steal a glance at the way he fills out his tailored shirt, the way the suspenders stretch over his wide shoulders, or the gleam I see in his stare.

Any positive thoughts I'm entertaining about this man are wrong.

Fool me once, shame on you.

Fool me twice, shame on me.

Chapter Two

Ricky

My smile twitches as Marilyn walks toward the front of the church, the eyes of many Riverbend residents shifting between her and those of us already at the altar. No doubt, many of the people sitting in the pews are thinking what I thought the day my little sister informed me she was dating my best friend. While my first reaction was disbelief, which morphed into shock and anger, I slowly realized what Devan obviously knew. Justin Sheers is a good guy. As he's my best friend since childhood, I couldn't come up with a better person for my sister to share the rest of her life with.

It is funny how the significance represented by the

numbers associated with our ages diminishes as we grow older. The gaps shrink as the years multiply.

Five years ago, when Devan graduated from high school, she and her friends seemed so much younger. I suppose that makes me an asshole for hooking up with Marilyn during that graduation party. We couldn't blame alcohol. It was something more basic, something that has existed since the beginning of time—desire, continuing from generation to generation and populating the earth.

After Marilyn and I did what we did, I was an ass. It hadn't occurred to me that I was Marilyn's first. The moment I realized that I was, I froze. Sure, she was beautiful and legal, but taking her virginity was more responsibility than I was prepared to accept. We agreed to keep what happened our secret—no strings attached.

I wasn't ready for the hostile aftermath. I suppose I should have been. What can I say? I'm a guy, and admitting feelings for my little sister's best friend was a hard no. Hurting her was never my intention. Due to our connection—Devan—avoiding each other was impossible. Over the years, we settled into an adversarial relationship. She never missed an opportunity to snap some smartass response whenever we were together. The thing is, I've grown not only to expect her zingers, but to look forward to them.

Last night at the rehearsal, I played along with her complaints about being paired with me. After all, I'm the best man and she's the maid of honor. The coupling should have been assumed before we listened to the minister's instructions.

For the sake of Justin and Devan, we agreed to play nice.

As she glides up the aisle, I can't help but scan from her dark hair, pulled up in a twist with glittery accessories, to her pleasing face and the way her pouty lips purse when she glances my way. My focus continues down her slender neck and to the way the clinginess of her long dress showcases her curves—curves that have grown over the last five years.

My circulation warms thinking about her aversion to me. For this one evening, she has no choice but to accept her role and mine. I nod slightly with a grin as she takes one last look in my direction and scrunches her adorable nose. If the congregation wasn't oohing and aahing over the flower girl, Justin's niece, I could laugh out loud.

The guests stand as the music changes.

Dad and Devin appear at the end of the aisle.

The happiness on my sister's face tells me what I knew as soon as I quit sulking over my best friend finding what I haven't—love. Devan glows as she holds on to Dad's arm and comes forward in her long white bridal gown.

The wedding occurs in a blur as I bear witness to the marriage of my sister to my best friend. Before I know it, the minister declares them husband and wife. The church erupts in applause as they kiss. My smile returns as the bride and groom walk down the aisle, I bend my right arm, and grin down at my partner for the night.

Marilyn's smile is forced as she places her hand on my arm, and she tips her chin higher.

"Maybe we should kiss, you know, see if they applaud again?" I whisper low into her ear.

Her face snaps toward mine. "Please don't make me sick. I've already had too much champagne."

My laugh comes from deep in my throat as we walk toward the back of the church. As soon as we cross the threshold, Marilyn lets go of my arm and hurries to Devan, wrapping her friend in a hug. My hand goes out to Justin. "It's official, asshole. You better treat my sister right."

His shoulders broaden and his neck straightens. "You know I will."

"I know." I pat his shoulder. "I'm still uncomfortable with it, but I know."

Our talk is cut short as Jill and Dax arrive—the last couple from the wedding party. They're followed by my parents and Justin's. Soon, we fall into line, Devan on my left and Marilyn on my right. One by one, the guests walk by. All the women hug my sister, and the men shake Justin's hand. The rest of us are met with the obligatory comments: beautiful wedding, you look nice, you clean up well. To hear the people of Riverbend, they aren't used to seeing me as anything other than Jack Dunn's son, a farmer.

That is changing.

I'm also not living in Riverbend any longer.

Since Mom and Dad sold our land to the Sheers, farming is no longer my livelihood; it's my hobby. I'm a semester into my bachelor's studies at Indiana University in Bloomington, majoring in economics and finance. With my associate's degree as a starting point, I'm over a decade older than many of my classmates, but I don't care. In two more years, I'll have my degree. Now that I'm knee-deep in classes, reading, and homework, I know this is the path I've always wanted.

As the guests make their way to the reception, the wedding party is herded back into the chapel for photographs. The photographer barks out orders, telling us where to stand.

"Ladies, place your hand on the shoulder of your partner. Devan and Justin, you're in the middle."

Craning my neck, I smirk toward Marilyn. "You can touch me. I won't bite."

"Don't get too comfortable," she says without a grin. "I may."

"Oh, interesting. I could be persuaded."

"Shut up and look at the camera."

Nearly an hour later, we pile into the back of a long limousine. Marilyn quickly sits at Devan's side and pulls Jill into her other side, leaving me sitting between Justin and Dax. Molly sits next to her dad.

The MC at the reception announces Molly first. Dax and Jill are the next to enter, hand in hand, Jill holding her bouquet high. I offer my hand to Marilyn, who looks away, pastes a smile on her lips, and walks at my side. The room cheers. The accolades grow louder as Devan and Justin enter to a chant of "Kiss, kiss."

"Too bad they didn't yell that for us," I say to Marilyn.

"That's not happening."

I'm not sure what makes me continue to tease—maybe it isn't teasing. I see her pouty lips and feel the fire beneath her soft skin. Marilyn has grown up since our one time together, and there is part of me that wants to investigate the woman she's become. It's the part of me that reacts to her smart comebacks. It's the part of me that literally screwed up five years ago.

Telling my body to forget this fiery brunette with the mesmerizing blue eyes is like telling my lips I no longer like ice cream.

That's it. I'm on a lactose-free diet.

Before the dinner, I stand and give my speech. The guests laugh as I give Justin the hundredth warning to take care of my little sister. Marilyn's speech is next, recounting Devan's and her friendship over the years. When she mentions their young childhood, I can't for the life of me remember Devan, Jill, or especially Marilyn as children.

Hell no.

When I wasn't looking and when I was, the three of them grew up.

My sister is no longer a kid. And without a doubt, Marilyn is definitely a woman.

Later that night, during the wedding party dance, I take Marilyn's hand and place my other one on her hip. The material of her dress is soft and shiny beneath my touch. "I'm living in Bloomington now."

Marilyn's blue eyes come in my direction and narrow, yet she doesn't respond.

"You're there, right?" I ask.

"I was. I'm doing my internship in Indianapolis."

My eyebrows shoot up. "Internship, with who?"

"Parker and Stevens."

"No shit?" I say, genuinely impressed. "They're one of the top wealth management firms in the country."

Marilyn's shoulders straighten. "You've heard of them?"

"As part of an assignment, I did research on different financial institutions in the state and beyond. Parker and Stevens was ranked highest for assets under management, individual client count, and clients per adviser."

Her cheeks rise as she grins. "They've also been in business for over seventy-five years."

"Maybe one day you can put in a good word for me."

Marilyn tilts her head. "Why would I do that?"

"Because you like me."

"Oh, is this more of the act we're doing for Devan and Justin?"

It is my turn to smile. "No, it's because we're both adults, and we can look beyond the past into the future."

She shakes her head. "If you want a good word before the clock strikes midnight, I might be able to help you out. After that, I'd say, remember me? I'm one of the no-strings girls from your past. If you wanted strings, you wouldn't have treated me the way you did."

One of...no, she isn't one of a long list.

Marilyn is the one I regret, not because she isn't everything I would want. Because she is the one I shouldn't want—the too-young friend of my little sister. Marilyn is the one I never should have touched and definitely never should have taken from what I did.

I notice the music has changed and others are joining us on the dance floor as Marilyn begins to back away,

I hold tight to her hand, stopping her escape. "Maybe it's not too late for strings."

Before I can make a convincing argument, she flashes her biggest and most insincere smile. "It's too late, Ricky. It was too late the morning you walked into your house and ignored me." She pulls her hand away and disappears into the sea of dancers.

Chapter Three

Marilyn

With my head held high, I slip into the ladies' bathroom. It isn't until I reach the safety and security of the stall that I let my face fall forward. Bolting the door, I grab handfuls of toilet paper, pressing the tissue to my eyes, willing my tears to stop, while simultaneously forbidding more from forming. My orbs sting from the combination of makeup and the salty evidence of my unwanted emotion.

I should have convinced Devan to select Jill as her maid of honor.

I shouldn't have slept with Ricky.

I never should have admitted that he hurt me. In all the years, I've never told him.

There are too many shoulds and shouldn'ts to count as I recall what it's like to be in Ricky's arms. I'm not thinking about what happened between us five years ago. My mind is too busy dealing with the dance we just shared, the touch of his hand to my waist and his strong, steady hold of my hand. I can't allow myself to entertain the way warmth radiated from his hard, toned body.

Ricky may have given up farming in pursuit of a career in finance, but over fifteen years of manual labor have left him with sculpted muscles that men in the cities pay personal trainers to create. Last night at the rehearsal, I failed at not noticing the bulge of his biceps beneath the hem of his short-sleeved shirt or the scroll of the tattoo that played peekaboo beneath the same sleeve.

Ricky has changed over the last half decade. While his body has gotten sharper, trimmed, and toned, the rough edges of the personality he once had have softened. I tell myself not to read too much into the way he stared when he asked about my internship, to ignore the soft suede of his eyes as his gaze locked on mine, and the genuine interest in his tone. That's easier than telling my body not to react to his presence.

Ricky may have been my first sexual encounter, but not my last. The list isn't excessive, but I've had enough experience to know that despite the pain that comes with the first time, Ricky has been a difficult act to follow. Maybe I've blown up his prowess in my mind. I can't be sure. I never will be able to be certain.

"Marilyn?"

I recognize Jill's voice. Inhaling, I work to regulate my voice. "I'm in here." One of my best friend's shoes comes into view, and I open the door.

Immediately, Jill tilts her head and her smile fades. "What's wrong?"

"Nothing," I say, inhaling, throwing the wad of tissue into the toilet, and flushing it down. Straightening my neck and squaring my shoulders, I turn to meet her gaze. "I'm great. How are you?"

Jill reaches for my hand and looks around the otherwise empty room. "What happened? Did Ricky say something to upset you?"

"He's been—" I hesitate as I retrieve my hand "—nice. He's made a few stupid cracks, but so have I."

"Mar, it's been five years. Think of it as water under the bridge or some stupid phrase my mom or your mom would say."

"After tonight, I won't need to see him again. I'm happy for Devan, but the constant combining of her friends and Justin's has been...a lot."

Jill scrunches her nose. "I was looking for you because Devan's about to do the bouquet toss."

I shake my head. "I'll let Molly or someone her age catch it."

"You can't do that. Superstition says whoever catches the bouquet marries next. You know Dax and Kandace won't let Molly marry until she's at least thirty. You would be..."

An old maid. The comment is on the tip of my tongue. Instead, I say, "I don't believe in superstitions."

Despite my objections, a few minutes later, Jill and I are watching the dance floor as Justin lifts the skirt of Devan's dress. The room erupts in laughter as he ducks beneath the layers of material, emerging with her garter between his teeth. The single men shout as they bounce off one another's shoulders. Ricky isn't the only male in this group who is still single. I spot men I've known since I was a child, ones I've seen more recently because of Devan and Justin. There's Galvin Mills. He's close to Ricky and Justin's age and a chef at Bynard's, one of the fanciest restaurants in the area. I also spot Harvey Russel and Nick Dancy. There are also younger men, all the way down in age to boys.

Justin turns around and stretches the garter like a rubber band. While most of the men reach for it, it lands solidly on the chest of a boy about three and a half feet tall. His round cheeks fill with color as the other men razz him about his plans to marry.

"Single ladies," the MC announces, "up to the dance floor."

When I don't move, Jill reaches for my arm. "Go on. You promised Devan you'd go out there after you bailed at my wedding."

I turn to see Devan's questioning stare on me.

"Fine, but I'm not catching it. Molly would be better for the little guy who caught the garter." Slowly, I make my way to the dance floor. Unlike the number of single men in Riverbend, the majority of the female population has either married or moved away. Lucky me, I'm back.

Devan's eyes twinkle as she scans the girls and a few ladies. As soon as she turns away, I hurry to the other side of the grouping, near the back, and away from where she saw me standing.

"One, two, three," Devan shouts. She flings the bouquet over her shoulder.

I blame it on years of softball. With no intention of catching the stupid flowers, as they came barreling at my face, I find my hands take on a life of their own. "Shit," I mutter under my breath.

Devan turns, her eyes wide as she sees me with the bouquet. Her fingertips go to her lips as her cheeks rise. "Marilyn, I thought you were the other way."

I lift the bouquet in the air. "I guess it's my lucky day."

"Will the catcher of the garter and the catcher of the bouquet please make their way to the dance floor?" the MC asks.

Inhaling, I look for my dance partner. With a shy grin, he comes my way. I scrunch down to his height. "Hi, I'm Marilyn."

"I'm Cole. You don't have to dance with me if you don't want to."

Despite the number of eyes upon us, I can't help but feel sorry for Cole. My smile grows. "I'd love to dance with you."

His smile widens. "I'm not very good at it."

"It's okay. We'll just hold hands and sway."

As the music starts, Cole's eyes meet my breasts. With pink in his cheeks, he looks up, having more courtesy than men twice or three times his age. In a nervous fit of him talking, I learn that Cole is nine years old, and his dad and Justin are friends. He is going into the fourth grade and can't wait to have Miss Dunn—he corrects himself to say Mrs. Sheers—as a teacher. He also confesses that he thinks Molly is cute, but she talks too much. I'm genuinely enjoying the mostly one-sided conversation when I feel a tap on my shoulder. Turning, I catch Ricky's gaze. Justin's niece Molly is at his side.

"We were wondering if we could cut in?" Ricky says with a grin.

I turn to Cole. "Would you be all right with switching partners?"

Cole swallows and nods.

Molly steps toward Cole, and they take each other's hands, swaying like he and I were moments ago.

In seconds, I'm back in Ricky's arms. His steady, strong grasp of my hand and the warmth of his palm on my lower back direct our steps as he leads me over the dance floor. Ricky's gaze skirts my breasts as he pulls me against him.

"If you're waiting for a thank-you, I think Cole was a better partner."

Ricky flinches as if I've slapped him. "I'm not happy with him cutting in. Officially, you're my partner for the night." Before I can say anything, he goes on, "I should have told you years ago, I'm sorry."

Inhaling, I lift my chin. "You're going to have to be more specific."

"Have I done that many things requiring forgiveness?"

"I don't have the list in front of me, but I'd venture to say it's longer than I can recount in one dance."

He shakes his head. "No, Marilyn. It's official wedding rules. All your dances are mine."

I look to the side and see Dax Richards dancing with his wife Kandace. Jill and Todd are also dancing.

"Apparently Dax and Jill didn't read the same rules you did."

He flashes a cheesy grin. "The wedding judges can deal with them. I'm only concerned that we keep up our side of the bargain."

The smart quips lower my defenses. "Fine. Which of your many offenses are you apologizing for?"

Ricky's shoulders stiffen beneath my touch. "Are you really going to make me say it?"

"If you're truly sorry, you'll say it."

He leans closer, his warm breath skirting over my neck and collarbone. "We agreed to no strings. That said, I never should have ghosted you after..."

My eyes close as I listen to his apology. He is right. That night long ago, we agreed to no strings. It made sense in my mind; it was the rest of me that felt rejected or abandoned. I've worked too hard to forget those feelings to have them resurface now.

There's no explanation or excuse in Ricky's apology, simply that he is sorry. Taking a deep breath, I lean away. The wedding guests around us are dancing and enjoying their own conversations. No one is paying attention to the two of us, just as no one paid attention to us five years ago.

"Will you accept my apology?"

I swallow the snide retort I'm used to giving him. "We've both grown up since then." I ask the question

I've always wanted to know the answer to. "Does Justin know?"

Ricky shakes his head.

"Anyone?"

"Did I brag about what happened? I didn't. If I would have told anyone, it would have been Justin." He shakes his head. "With as close as you and Devan are...I mean, you were planning on being roommates at Ball State...I didn't say a word."

My thoughts go back to that time. "She's one of my best friends. It was tough not to tell her, so I just let her know I hate you."

His lips curl. "You hate me."

While Ricky didn't ask it as a question, I reply, "Hate is a strong word. I'm not as romantic as Devan or as satisfied as Jill, but it's taken me a while to be strong enough to dance with you."

He shakes his head. "You're strong, Marilyn, and sexy." He runs his hand up my side. His touch isn't inappropriate, yet it borders on the too familiar. "You're also damn smart. You wouldn't have gotten the internship at Parker and Stevens if you weren't. You've known that you wanted out of this small town. Back then, I thought this was where I wanted to spend my life."

"You've changed your mind?"

"It's not like Bloomington is far away, but I'm

liking my classes. I have a part-time job that sucks, but that's all part of growing up and moving on. Quite the epiphany for a thirty-three-year-old man. It obviously took me longer to come to that conclusion than it did you."

"They say males mature slower."

Ricky scoffs. "Friends?"

"I can say I don't hate you anymore. Friends is taking it a bit far."

"I guess I'll settle for whatever I can get."

Chapter Four

Marilyn
A year and a half later

Stomping the snow from my boots, I look around the small café as the delicious aromas fill my senses. At this time of day, most of the tables and booths are occupied. I'm relieved to see my friend already has a table. By the time I reach Jill, my gloves are off and stuffed into my pockets. While we don't get a lot of snow in Indianapolis, we can still experience the arctic freeze that accompanies the new year. In the last twenty-four hours, the temperature has dropped into the low twenties, making the two-block walk from my office long enough to lose the feeling in my fingers and toes. Shrugging off my long coat, I lay it over the chair to my side and sit across from Jill.

It's hard to believe that we've been friends for nearly two decades. The talkative girls in grade school are still talking and laughing twenty years later. Only our surroundings have changed. No longer living in Riverbend, we both made it to the big city of Indianapolis. It isn't New York or LA, but compared to our roots, it's metropolitan, especially the northside where we both work.

Jill giggles as I take the seat. "I'm glad you could make it."

"Tax season is about to start, and I'll be swamped." I exhale. "The fun of a new year."

Our conversation halts as the waitress approaches. "Can I get you something to drink?"

As I rub my hands together, I see Jill's cup of hot chocolate. It's definitely a day for warm drinks. Smiling, I reply, "Coffee, hot coffee."

"Coming right up."

Jill lifts her cup. "I can't believe we both have jobs a few blocks from each other."

I couldn't agree more. While I've made new friends at Parker and Stevens and others from my gym and apartment complex, old friends are special. "And we haven't met up since before the holidays. How is your family?"

"Good." She rolls her eyes. "It's always a fight over whose house we'll stay at when we visit. I'd rather be at my parents', and Todd wants to be at his parents'. The thing is, the Blakelys haven't changed Todd's room since he was in high school. Oh, they replaced his twin bed with a full."

I scrunch my nose. "A full?"

Jill nods. "When you're used to a king-sized, a full might as well be a twin. And we have to go back next weekend for Todd's sister's daughter's birthday."

"Where are you going to stay?"

"My parents' house."

"What about your old room?" I ask.

"Oh, it's a perfectly fine guest room with a queen-sized bed. My mom has no problem with 'out with the old and in with the new.'"

I laugh as the waitress arrives with my coffee. The ceramic mug warms my fingers. "I wanted to see more people in Riverbend," I confess. "But since I could only get a few days off, Mom had a million things planned. I didn't even get a chance to see Devan."

"Oh, she and Justin have made their farmhouse so cute. Talk about 'out with the old and in with the new.' It looks totally different than it did when we were kids."

"I saw it last summer. They weren't finished with the kitchen yet. I know Devan spent her summer vacation painting and changing the landscaping. I'm not sure how I would feel about living in and changing my childhood home."

Jill nods. "The Dunns have been super supportive, according to Devan. They want her and Justin to make the house feel like their home, not like they're living in Devan's old house."

"I'm not sure my mom would be that open to change." I lift the menu. "It doesn't matter. Melissa is graduating high school this year, and Marcus is settled in Chicago. I don't see my parents moving anywhere."

"I can't believe your little sister is graduating high school. I suppose that's how Justin felt about Devan before they connected. I mean, in my mind, Melissa is still a little girl."

I shake my head. "She's all grown up. And she's been accepted to Purdue."

"Oh," Jill exclaims. "Traitor."

I can't help but laugh. The state of Indiana is divided into two camps—IU or Purdue. It doesn't matter whether the person attended one school or the other or they simply live in Indiana. Everyone has an opinion. And considering Jill graduated with her bachelor's degree and master's degree from IU, she has the right to favor her alma mater.

"According to Missy, the Mitchell E. Daniels, Jr. School of Business is the best in the state."

Jill purses her lips. "She has a right to her opinion, even if it's wrong."

After the waitress takes our order, I ask Jill about her job. She's the human resources manager for a law firm up the street, here in Carmel.

"I love it," she says, her smile beaming. "I've been talking to Todd about going back to school." She sighs. "I think I want to take the LSAT."

"Become a lawyer?"

Jill nods. "I know by some Riverbend rule, I should be popping out babies by now, but honestly, Todd is so busy with his firm, neither one of us is ready for kids. After spending the last six months in the law firm, I want to do more."

"I think that's great."

"And your job?" she asks.

"I love the firm. It's growing, and I feel like I came along at the right time. Wealth management is the new must-have. The demographics of Carmel and, really, all north Indy is ripe for our services."

"Well," Jill says, "when Todd and I have any wealth to manage, we'll come to you."

We both grow silent as our lunches are delivered. Once the waitress is gone, Jill lowers her voice. "How was your date with the guy from the gym?"

"T.J.," I say, shaking my head. "It was blah. I can't

even say it was bad. He was boring—oh, unless I wanted to talk about him."

"I don't know if I could date. Todd and I have been together forever. It would be awkward."

"It is. I mean, T.J. is nice to watch on the treadmill, but it only took a drink and an appetizer for me to start making excuses for an early retreat."

"Maybe you need to get to know him better."

"In a twenty-minute span of time, I learned about his degree from Hanover College. He then spent a gap year abroad and speaks four languages. Oh, and his parents own a trucking company, so he's a trust-fund baby and only works because it's expected of him, not because he needs to."

Jill stifles a laugh. "He had me at four languages. What about Bryce?"

I shake my head. "Ship has sailed. I mean, it's awkward when we are put together on projects at work, but we're both good with moving on. Sometimes you just know it's not meant to be."

It seems that I'm better at knowing when it's not meant to be than when it is.

Forcing a grin, I go on, "I give up on the dating scene. I think I'll get three or four cats and spend my nights with Ben and Jerry."

"Ben and Jerry are good company, but I prefer Häagen-Dazs."

"Because they speak other languages?"

We both laugh.

By the time our lunch is finished, we both need to head back to our offices. With my long wool coat buttoned, my gloved hands buried deep in my pockets, and my boots treading carefully on the frozen sidewalk, I make my way through the frosted air to Parker and Stevens. Each breath forms a small cloud of condensation. By the time I step into the reception air, I relish the warmth.

"Ms. James," Klara, one of the receptionists, says, lifting a piece of paper. "You received a call while you were away."

Removing a glove, I reach for the paper. "Thank you." I stare down at the name and number. "Rich Dunn?"

"Yes, ma'am. That was what he said. He'd like you to call him back when you have a moment."

Rich can't be Ricky, can it?

"Is he a client?" I ask.

"His name doesn't match with anyone in our system."

"Did he say what he wanted?" I ask, still contemplating that Rich Dunn is actually Ricky Dunn.

"No. He only asked that I relay his message for you to return his call."

"Thank you," I say again, staring down at the name.

Rich.

Ricky.

No. It couldn't be.

Curiosity gets the better of me by the time I make it back to my office. It's a small room with a small window, but it is an office, complete with a door. That's a step up from the cubicle I inhabited while working as an intern. The nameplate outside the door reads *Marilyn James, Wealth Adviser*. Whenever I see the plate, I smile. My love life may be nonexistent, but I have accomplished a few rungs on the ladder, climbing to success.

After hanging my coat on a coat tree, I settle behind my desk. If I knew for sure that the message was from Ricky, I could call him back on my cell phone. If this isn't him, I don't necessarily want a stranger to know my private number.

Dunn.

How many people have that last name?

The two of us haven't spoken since Devan and Justin's wedding.

Lifting the receiver, I hit the numbers on the paper.

The call rings twice, before I hear his voice.

"Marilyn, thanks for calling me back."

Ricky.

I don't know if I'm happy or agitated.

Why call me at work?

Chapter Five

Rich/aka Ricky
Earlier

Even the closed door won't deafen the vibrating bass shaking the walls of our apartment. There's no sense telling Max to turn down the music. I learned that fight wasn't worth my breath. Besides, I've rarely won that argument since we first moved in together. Truth be told, I prefer the music to what it's hiding. Max Brenner and I met at Foot Locker, the store in the mall where I work part time. While I'm ready to leave the days of selling athletic shoes behind, Max is living his best life.

The idea of living together came from me. Max, five years younger than me, constantly complained about living with his parents. My apartment had two bedrooms, and a roommate meant half the expenses. I hadn't thought the whole thing through. Cramming extra classes into each semester, as well as taking summer courses, meant I finished my degree a semester early. When combined with a part-time job, it left little to no time for much of anything else.

Max makes up for my lack of socialization.

That is why, if I were a cartoon character, there would currently be smoke coming from my ears. In the three-dimensional world, my temples are pounding in time with the bass. The music is Max's way of letting me know that I'd rather hear the booming sound than the noises coming from his bedroom. From the glittery purse and strappy high heels in the living room, I know he's got some girl in there.

Her name, I have no idea.

I gave up trying to keep track a long time ago.

Max practices what he calls free love, as if he should have been born fifty years ago. He would have made the perfect hippie in my grandparents' generation.

Lying back on my bed, I flop my arm over my forehead and stare up at the ceiling. My degree is complete, and I want a real job, one utilizing that piece of paper. It's my fault for thinking the job offers would roll in. I should have started looking earlier. The thing is, that after eighteen months of watching every dime, I want more.

I close my eyes and let out a long breath.

More.

I want more.

First on my list is a house or apartment for myself.

Second is a life beyond school and work.

Fuck, I'm thirty-five years old, and I have little to show for my life.

When my parents sold our land in Riverbend—a small town in southwest Indiana—they gave a healthy chunk of the profits to me. After all, over the last ten years, I'd put in as much, if not more work than my dad, keeping the farm going. That nest egg is smaller than it was when I first put it in my bank account, but I've managed to keep most of it by watching my expenses.

To say I'm tired of living whatever this life is with Max and his parade of women is an understatement. I'm ready for a life.

My life.

I must fall asleep, because when I open my eyes, it's morning and the apartment is peacefully quiet.

"Fuck," I murmur as I roll off the bed and reach for my phone. In my head, I'm doing mental gymnastics.

What day is it?

What time is it?

Am I late for class?

Am I scheduled to work?

Running my fingers through my hair, I concentrate on the screen.

Shit. It's noon on Tuesday.

I remember that classes are done; I have my degree. That is, until I start working on my master's degree. I'm not scheduled at the store until the three-o'clock-to-closing shift. I'm about to exit my room when I see the name of a firm I have been dreaming of working for on an email: Parker and Stevens.

Preparing myself for a "Dear John" in the form of a hiring, not dating, response, I click the email open. My eyes bug as I read the email not once, not twice, but three times.

Mr. Dunn,

Thank you for your time with our interview procedure. Herold Parker and Ralph Stevens would like to extend an invitation to the next phase of our process, a dinner with our partners and select members of our team.

Location: Hotel Carmichael

Cocktails: 6:30 p.m.

Dinner: 7:30 p.m.

Please RSVP by Tuesday at 5:00 p.m. We apologize for the short notice; the holidays delayed our invitation.

The partners would like to get to know you in a less formal atmosphere. A plus-one is acceptable and encouraged.

Contact Tillie Johnson at this email address with any questions and your confirmation.

Thank you,

Tillie Johnson

Assistant to Ralph Stevens, Partner

"Fuck," I say louder, looking around for a camera or something to indicate this is a prank. No cameras. I open my bedroom door. Max's door is partially ajar. The disaster left behind by Tornado Max is threatening to invade our hallway. However, judging by the lack of noise, he and whoever was with him are gone.

I think about the email.

It is dated yesterday. Somehow with my work schedule and the distraction of Max's music last night, I must not have seen it.

RSVP by Tuesday.

"Shit, shit..." My mind goes in a million different directions. This is the cherry on the top of a sundae job. The dream firm, the one I've been wanting ever since Marilyn mentioned their name.

Marilyn.

I search my contacts for my sister's number. Devan's a seventh-grade science teacher in Riverbend. Her ringer is probably off, but I hit the call button anyway.

"Ricky? Is everything okay?"

"You answered."

Devan laughs. "I'm eating lunch at my desk. You caught me. What's up?"

"Does Marilyn work for the firm Parker and Stevens? I remember she had an internship there."

"Why do you want to know where Marilyn works?"

"Dev, just tell me."

"You never told me the two of you kissed."

"Yeah." That was our cover story. "None of your business." Now I sound like a ten-year-old fighting with his sister. "I have a third interview with Parker and Stevens, and I wanted to talk to Marilyn if she works there."

"She does. Do you need her number?"

I'm about to say yes. Before the word materializes, I suddenly worry she won't take my call. "No. If she works there, I'll call her at work."

"Okay. The bell is about to ring. I have to go."

"Thanks, Devan." I disconnect the call.

The last time I spoke to Marilyn was at Devan's wedding. She said she didn't hate me. I'm not sure that means she will be willing to help me, but I need to find out. This dinner could be the key to me getting out of this apartment and a real life.

Checking Parker and Stevens's website, I find what I could have found without calling Devan. Marilyn's picture, a short biography, and the title Wealth Consultant – Fiduciary are staring back at me. For a moment, I take in her photo. In a business jacket, she looks professional and as pretty as she did at the wedding.

How had I not paid more attention to the blue of her eyes?

Taking a breath, I chastise myself. I already fucked things up with Marilyn once. I need to keep this professional.

When I call the number on the screen, I'm told she is out of the office. I leave a message.

Now, I must wait.

I'm supposed to RSVP by five o'clock tonight.

After a cup of coffee, I get into the shower, contemplating going to the dinner solo. It wouldn't be so bad, would it? Why would the partners suggest a plus one? As the hot water rains down on me, I answer my own question. They want to know more about the applicants, such as if they're stable and in a committed relationship. They hired Marilyn, and she isn't married.

That thought is like a punch in my gut. I should have asked Devan that question. Maybe she is married. Why didn't I ask? Her name on the website is listed as Marilyn James. That means she's not married. Or she kept her maiden name.

My head is swirling with these new thoughts.

Surely Devan would have said if Marilyn is in a relationship or married. Then again, why would she?

My internal debate ends with the ringing of my phone.

I turn off the water and reach for a towel.

The name "Parker and Stevens Wealth Management" is on the screen.

Taking a deep breath, I answer the call. "Marilyn, thanks for calling me back."

"Ricky?" Marilyn asks. "What's with the new name?"

Oh, I forget that people from my past aren't used to the name Rich.

I trap the phone between my shoulder and chin as I wrap a towel around my waist. At the sound of her voice, I remember the way she looked at me at Devan's wedding, the way the dress accentuated her curves. Trying not to think about her breasts pushed against me when we danced, I work to keep my voice even.

"First, thanks for calling me back. I wasn't sure if you would."

"That's why you tried to be sneaky with your name."

A laugh bubbles from my throat. "I'm not exactly sneaky. Rich and Ricky are both short for Richard."

"So is Dick."

My cheeks rise. "Yeah, my headhunter thought Rich would look better on résumés."

"I don't know, Dick Dunn would certainly catch people's attention. Why did you call me at work? Do you need a wealth manager?"

"No," I scoff. Hardly. Making it to the next paycheck is more my speed. Instead of saying that, I reply, "It's part business and part personal."

"I'm curious," Marilyn says. "What's the business and what's the personal?" She pauses. "I have a meeting with a client in ten minutes."

So much for chitchat. "Remember that I went back to college?"

"I remember."

"I loaded up on the hours and completed my bachelor's in December. I thought I might see you in Riverbend over the holidays."

"Couldn't get a lot of time off. Business, personal," she prompts.

"Work, well...that's why I'm calling. I've been on

more than a few interviews." My mouth goes dry as I say what I've practiced. "One position is with Parker and Stevens."

"Oh."

I was hoping for a more enthusiastic response, but I continue, "It's a starting position, one in research, but it's a foot in the door. I'm not ready to be a fiduciary yet. I'm hoping to work as an underling and, at the same time, take classes toward my master's degree." I don't pause, afraid if I do, Marilyn will cut me off. "The thing you might already know is that these entry positions are relatively new, and Parker and Stevens has a huge selection of applicants. I was hoping that maybe I could stand out above the rest with your help."

"My help?"

Biting the bullet, I spit out my question, "Marilyn, will you be my date for the dinner with the partners? It's only for one date and no strings." When she doesn't respond, I add, "It's a recruit dinner. There will be twenty of us there vying for an undisclosed number of openings. I was hoping—"

"When is the dinner?"

Inhaling, I take a much-needed breath. A question is better than a flat-out no. "This Friday."

Marilyn coughs. "This Friday, as in today is Tuesday?"

"That's the way it works. I only received the email

with the invitation yesterday. I didn't see it until today," I admit. "It said something about a delay with the holidays. It asked about a plus-one, and I thought of you."

"Not to be rude," Marilyn says.

I brace myself for her to be just that. Here it comes, her smartass comment.

She goes on, "Why me?"

Okay, not what I expected. "You know the partners. You work for them. This is one friend helping the other."

"Hmm."

Taking a deep breath, I lay it on the line. "Help a friend out."

Chapter Six

Marilyn

A friend.

I wonder what's wrong with me. Am I a masochist when it comes to men? Or is it only with Ricky? If I say yes to his dinner invitation, am I opening the dam I've built, block by block, over the years, the one that is supposed to keep the feelings about Ricky safely concealed far behind it? Then again, if I say no, am I allowing a mistake from the past, from both of our pasts, to influence the future?

"I went to a similar dinner a few years ago," I volunteer. "They're looking for stability, not a one-night stand."

Why did I say that?

Ricky is quiet for a moment. "We could fake it."

"Fake what?" My circulation warms.

"Fake a stable relationship. I mean, we've known each other since you were a kid."

Great.

"You weren't exactly an adult twenty years ago."

"Fuck, Marilyn, you know what I mean. We come from the same hometown. We can make this seem like we've been together for a while. I could even say you're my inspiration for applying to Parker and Stevens."

"I don't know..." I'm suddenly worried about who will be at the dinner. My social status isn't a common conversation topic, but then again, during my time at the firm, I haven't exactly acted like I'm in a serious long-term relationship.

My thoughts are going a million miles a minute when Ricky's voice registers. "The dinner is on Friday. How about meeting me for a casual dinner on Thursday, and we can work out our cover story?"

There is something in his voice, comfort that comes with knowing the other person. It's not that anything between us deserves that level of contentment, yet I think I hear it. My bravery sparks to life. "It sounds like you're assuming I will say yes." A grin he can't see curls my lips. The longer I ruminate on this idea, the more the possibility of playing this role with him tantalizes my skin, sending much-needed endorphins through my bloodstream.

"If the firm is looking for stability," Ricky says, "and I arrive sans a plus one, will it affect my likelihood of being hired?"

"Legally, it's not a requirement for hire."

"Did you have a plus-one?" he asks.

I take a deep breath, thinking of Bryce. "Yeah, it wasn't fake. It also didn't last."

"But it could have helped with your hire?"

"I had completed my internship. Mr. Parker and Mr. Stevens knew my work ethic and could judge my experience."

"Again, you played the game. That's what I want to do."

With me.

"Unless," Ricky says, the confidence in his tone wavering. "Unless they know you're not in a relationship...or maybe you are. I'm sorry. Fuck, Marilyn, I should have led with that question. I didn't mean to step on some other guy's toes. If you're seeing someone..."

I don't want to admit that my romantic status is less than nonexistent. Unless my vibrator counts. Since it never takes me to dinner, and I'm the one who pays for the batteries...

"Oh shit."

I jump in. "No, that's not it. I don't work day-today with the partners. They have no idea of what my personal life involves."

"So, this could work?"

I'm probably going to regret my decision. Nevertheless, I set aside that thought as I blurt out my answer, "I'll do it."

"Fuck? Really? You're not trying to get back at me for being an asshole?"

"You admitted that at Devan's wedding, but it wouldn't hurt for you to worry about my sincerity throughout the partners' dinner."

Ricky scoffs. "Thursday, to set our story..."

"Matt the Miller's Tavern in City Center. Do you know the place?"

"I do. Six thirty?"

There are probably a hundred reasons not to do this, but I don't let my thoughts dwell on them. "Sounds good."

"Marilyn?"

I swallow. "Yes?"

"Thank you."

Nodding, I exhale. "See you Thursday. No strings," I say, reminding him of his proposal.

"No strings."

I hang up the call before Ricky can say anything else, close my eyes, and tip my forehead to the surface of my desk. What the heck have I just done?

My first instinct is to call Jill, but the tiny clock on the bottom of my computer screen tells me it's about time for my upcoming meeting. All work and no play have most definitely narrowed my perspective on life and love.

No.

These two evenings with Ricky aren't about love.

Friendship. Yes.

After all, friendship would be better than despising him every time we're forced to see each other. Time heals wounds—that's what my mom always says.

Could it be that I don't hate Ricky Dunn, but hate that he hurt me? If that's the case, perhaps my loathing has been my defense mechanism, my go-to in a way, to avoid future disappointment.

Or maybe taking a few psychology courses throughout my college career has me overanalyzing. It could also be that I have too much time on my hands, time to be rational.

That reasoning is well and good on a Tuesday at work or even during Wednesday night when home alone. However, as I park outside the restaurant in City Center with my heart thumping a rhythm in my ears and the difficulty I'm experiencing filling my lungs with sufficient air, I'll go out on a limb and hypothesize that rational thinking has left the building and irrational thinking has taken over.

I take one last look at my reflection in the rearview mirror.

"This isn't a date," I say audibly as I dig in my purse for my lip balm. Yes, it's slightly shaded, but only a little. My eyeliner from this morning is mostly gone, and I'm still wearing my slacks and blouse from the office.

While I'd toyed with the idea of going back to my apartment for a refresh after work, I ran out of time. My last two meetings went longer than planned, and now, I find myself sitting in my car, condensation forming on the insides of the windows as I regret my acceptance of Ricky's request. A quick look at my watch tells me I'm already five minutes late.

Not enough time to cancel.

Taking a deep breath, I open the car door. Over the last few days, the temperatures have risen to the comfy upper thirties. After the earlier cold spell, as I step from the car, the air feels almost tepid.

I take in the surroundings. During the warmer seasons, people would be out and about. The fountain outside the front doors is dry. In the summer, it's filled with water, illuminated by colorful lights. High above, darkness fills the winter sky, making the sign above the restaurant bright against the building.

When I open the front door, the sound of voices fills my ears as the aroma of delicious food tickles my senses, causing my stomach to rumble. The salad I ate for lunch seems like a long time ago. I scan the front room, looking for the boy from my childhood.

My breathing hitches and my focus narrows as I take in the man he's become. It's not that I don't recognize Ricky; it's that since Devan's wedding, he's changed, matured, aged—like a fine wine.

No longer perpetually tousled by the wind and elements, his light-brown hair is longer on top than I recall and styled—wavy on top and short on the sides. A shadow of beard growth lines his chiseled jaw, neatly trimmed, leaving his cheeks and his neck smooth. His wide shoulders are covered by a white button-down shirt, the sleeves rolled near his elbows. My gaze goes to where the shirt is tucked into a faded pair of denim jeans. Not the kind he used to wear while working on the farm. These appear better fitting, as demonstrated by the way they hug his ass.

"May I help you?" the hostess asks, bringing me back to reality.

"No, I see my..."

Date?

Friend?

Person I swore to hate forever?

"...my friend," I say, swallowing, despite the sudden dryness of my mouth. The hostess nods, allowing me passage.

As I walk into the bar, Ricky turns. There's a glint in his brown eyes. Small lines form in the corners as his cheeks rise and lips curl into a grin. Stepping from the barstool, he comes toward me.

For a moment, I stop, unsure of the next move.

This isn't scripted, as our interactions were during the wedding. And after years of dreading and avoiding him, I'm at a loss for how to react.

He stops mere inches away, the fresh, clean scent of his cologne mingling with the various delicious aromas. He lifts his arms, and I'm unsure how we should greet each other. I tilt my head and offer a lopsided grin. "You're not going to hug me, are you?"

Chapter Seven

Ricky

I can't hold back my smile. Marilyn James actually showed. If I were a betting man, I would have said the odds of her coming here tonight were against me. Seeing her snarky smile and the gleam in her soft blue orbs, I'd gladly lose that bet to have her here now. "I'm glad you showed," I say honestly, letting my arms drop to my sides.

"You're not going to hug me, are you?"

Was I about to hug her?

I feel the heat coming to my face. No matter how self-assured I act around others, there's something about Marilyn that sees through the bullshit. Avoiding her comment about the hug, I motion toward the bar, to where I was sitting. "Come. I have a stool for you.

They said there was a forty-minute wait for a table. I hope you don't mind waiting here."

Marilyn shakes her head and loosens the knot of the sash keeping her wool coat closed. Beneath the bulk of the winter covering, she unveils her light-colored blouse and slacks. While not intentionally revealing, I notice the way the neckline dips over her voluptuous breasts and the taper of her waist as the black material covers her long legs.

Her voice pulls me from my trance. "This is good. I'm sorry I'm late. Busy day."

"I want to hear all about your job. However, I'm warning you, if you tell me it's a terrible place to work, I'll be heartbroken."

She drapes her coat over the back of the stool and secures her purse beneath the bar on one of those little hooks. I can't help but continue to scan her, from her long dark hair to the toes of her boots. The little girl who used to hang out with Devan has grown up and grown out in all the right places. As she takes a seat, I inhale the slight sweetness of her perfume.

"Would you like a drink?" I ask.

Marilyn eyes the glass of beer before me. "What are you drinking?"

"It's a local craft beer, tall blond."

She smiles. "Good to know you prefer tall blonds."

My smile returns. "When it comes to beer, I'm

partial to blonds and ambers. When it comes to real life, I've always had a thing for brunettes."

Her eyes open wide. "Are we working on our script?"

"No, Marilyn, that's not pretend." I lean back and make a point of staring into her eyes. "I'd be remiss if I didn't tell you how pretty you look." I shake my head. "And how amazing I think it is that you've accomplished all that you have. I know I'm a little late to this world, but the truth is, I want it."

Marilyn's shoulders seem to relax.

The bartender appears before us. "Would you like a drink?" she asks Marilyn.

"A tall blond," she says with a smile and a sideways glance in my direction.

"I didn't know you liked beer."

"I'm not picky. My indulgence of choice is ice cream, not alcohol. But I'm not against a drink or two."

"I heard stories about Devan's bachelorette party."

She takes a deep breath before covering her face with her hands. "Oh, don't remind me." As she drops her hands, her cheeks glow with a hue of pink. "I've officially sworn off cheap wine for the rest of my life." Her smile grows. "Now, wine that doesn't come in a box, I'm still willing to partake in. In moderate amounts."

"I remember Devan being a little green that next morning."

Marilyn arches her eyebrow. "And you, Ricky Dunn, have never had too much to drink. What about Justin's bachelor party?"

"Oh, I was perfectly sober."

She hums and tilts her head.

"Until I wasn't. I couldn't let my best friend get married without a party."

The bartender sets Marilyn's glass of beer on a napkin in front of us. "Would you like anything else? Something to eat?"

It's my turn to lift a brow toward Marilyn. She shakes her head. "We're good for now."

"Let me know," the bartender says with a smile.

"I think you have an admirer," Marilyn says as she lifts her glass.

My gaze goes to the woman behind the bar and back to the one sitting at my side. "Would you believe me if I said I've been out of the dating scene for so long, I think my radar is broken? Because if you think she's sending something my way, I'm totally not picking it up."

She lifts her glass. "To your future."

Our glasses clink, and we each take a drink. Setting down my beer, I bite the bullet. "I know I told you at the wedding, but I'm sorry for the way I closed you out." Marilyn's smile fades, and I immediately regret bringing up the subject. "I may have been older than you, but that didn't mean I was more..."

As I struggle for the next word, Marilyn says, "Mature?"

"I'll take it. Guilty as charged. There's something about staying in Riverbend that hinders a person's ability to grow up."

"People grow up in Riverbend. I didn't want that, but I don't think less of those who do."

Exhaling, I sit straighter. "I'm not dissing people like Justin and Devan. Hell, she's my sister, and he's my best friend. If anything, I think Devan made Justin grow up. It's crazy to say, but before they got involved, Justin was like me."

"What is that?"

This is the most honest I've been with anyone in years. "A boat lost on the sea. A dandelion turned to seed and floating in the air."

Her smile returns. "I didn't know you were this deep."

"Oh, I'm not. It's that I appreciate you helping me, and if we're going to make this seem legitimate, I thought the best thing was to come clean. Before Devan, I wondered if Justin was as sick of farming as I was. Every now and again, he'd make a comment." I lift my beer. "He wasn't tired of farming. He was just untethered."

"Now he's tethered—tied down?"

I shake my head. "That's not a bad thing. I mean, it sounds bad." I chuckle. "But for Justin, it's given him the focus and drive he didn't have." I sit taller. "He's kicking ass with ethanol. And don't tell Devan, but he's even made a few comments about being ready for kids."

Marilyn's eyes grow wide. "I'm not sure Devan is ready."

"That's why you can't tell her. He doesn't want to pressure her. They've got something that's..." I inhale again "...it's cool."

"What about you?" she asks.

"What about me?"

"Are you still a boat or dandelion puff?"

"No." I take a moment, giving her question consideration. "For the first time in my life, I think I'm on the right track. I mean, even after Vincennes, going back to Riverbend and farming was expected. You know, Dad took over Granddad's farm. I was next. This, getting my degree and looking for more than a job, a career...it feels right."

"Tell Justin that farming isn't a real job."

I take a sip of my beer. "That's not what I mean.

What about you? You didn't have a drive to return to our small hometown."

"No," she says and sighs. "That doesn't mean that sometimes I don't miss it, the people, the closeness, the support. It's different out here."

"Do you want to go back?"

"Oh, God no."

A laugh comes from my throat. "That's what I expected."

"But if we're both being honest, it gets lonely out here. You know how at home, when you walk down Main Street or go into the Main Street Diner...?"

I do know. "Yes, five to six mornings a week, like clockwork, there was a standing breakfast at the diner. The table would be filled with three or twelve men. We shot the shit and chowed down like there was no tomorrow."

"Do you have that here?"

"No. I have other things."

"Your degree," she says.

"And a feeling of self-worth that I lacked before."

Marilyn's smile grows. "I see that. It looks good on you."

"I was preparing all day for you to give me shit."

"Maybe I've matured too. Parker and Stevens is a good place to work. The position you're applying for used to be staffed by interns." She lowers her voice. "In other words, I did the work for free."

"I can't really afford free."

"Over the last few years, things have changed. If you get hired, there's a good chance that they'll offer you a stipend to continue your education."

"I have already applied for my master's. I'm scheduled to take the GMAT in a few weeks."

"Really?" she asks. "Oh my God, that test was worse than a million internships."

"Thanks."

She reaches out and covers my hand with hers. The warmth flows from where we touch throughout my body. As I look down, Marilyn lifts her hand.

"Sorry."

I don't know if she's apologizing for the touch or for scaring the shit out of me about the Graduate Management Admissions Test. "Don't be."

"I could help you with what questions to expect."

"You'd be willing to do that?"

She smirks. "A continuation of that Riverbend camaraderie."

"Well, we have been dating..." I leave the statement open, wondering where she'll take it.

"Off and on."

"That could work." I broaden my grin. "Tell me,

what do I need to know about my off-and-on, not-on-relationship. Tell me something only your boyfriend would know."

Chapter Eight

Marilyn

Something only my boyfriend would know.

My mind is blank.

Ricky nudges me with his shoulder. "I can go first."

"Good, because I'm currently floundering."

Tiny dimples appear in his cheeks as his smile grows. "I drink my coffee black, and I've been told I snore."

"I don't snore," I say. "And coffee with cream, not milk. Vanilla-flavored is even better."

"Now we're getting somewhere." He eyes the partially filled glass in front of me. "And you drink beer, good wine, but prefer ice cream. Flavor?"

"Caramel is the best, but few places make it well. My grandma made homemade caramel ice cream. We used to hand-spin it in an old bucket. There was ice and salt around the silver center."

Ricky's stare intensifies, his brown orbs sparkling.

"What?" I ask.

"That...what you were just saying. You really meant it. I could see and hear how happy those memories made you."

Nodding, I look down and back up, meeting his gaze. "Do you have memories that make you happy?"

"Yeah." He lifts his chin and purses his lips. "I have no complaints about anything from my childhood. I think everyone is supposed to have some trauma that shapes them or some shit. If I did, I blocked it out." His eyes open wide. "Devan. Yeah, she's my trauma."

"Devan was your trauma?" I ask, holding back a laugh.

"Now, hear me out. Imagine you're a ten-year-old kid. Life is going great. You have all your parents' attention, baseball, football, friends, woods to explore, fields to wander..."

"Living the dream."

"Exactly," Ricky replies. "And then, out of nowhere, this tiny pink, crying, diaper-soiling troll comes into your home, and your world is never the same."

"I can't wait to tell Devan that description."

"No," he says quickly. "This is secret boyfriend-girlfriend stuff. You can't tell anyone else."

"Oh, those are the rules?" I'm not sure if it's the beer or the company, but my dread leading up to this evening has disappeared.

"You have siblings. How much older are you than your sister?"

"Eight years, but Marcus came first. I don't really remember life without all of us around."

"You are definitely Marcus's trauma."

I shake my head.

Ricky leans closer, the warmth of his arm radiating to mine. "You're telling me you had no life-changing trauma?"

My lips come together. "Not in my childhood." I lift my eyebrows, ready to accuse Ricky of being my life-changing trauma. It wasn't the sex. I'd been a willing participant. It was the aftermath.

He stares for a moment before saying, "Maybe we should change the subject."

"Probably a good idea."

Could he read my thoughts?

Ricky's phone vibrates. After he looks at the screen, his smile returns. "Saved by the buzzer. Our table is ready." He lifts his hand, signaling to the bartender.

As I reach for my purse, Ricky shakes his head. "I asked you to meet tonight to work on our plan. Tonight is on me."

"I can pay for myself."

"I'm sure you can." He lowers his chin and widens his brown eyes. "Please, Marilyn. You're doing me a favor."

Against my better judgment, I acquiesce.

At our table, he asks me more questions. "If your significant other were to plan the perfect date, what would it be?" When I don't answer, he offers, "Jetting to Paris, dinner, and a walk around the Eiffel Tower?"

I shake my head. "I'm much simpler."

"Tell me."

My lips curl at the idea. "I've never planned my own date, but if I did, I'd say dinner, but not at a restaurant. A home-cooked meal that includes some of my favorite dishes." I giggle. "Here's a secret—I'm not the world's healthiest eater. Those dishes would include fettuccine or spaghetti."

"Carbs."

I nod. "And dessert."

"Caramel ice cream."

"Or cheesecake. No fruit, just a thick slice of cheesecake."

The rest of the evening, we spend talking about mutual friends and avoiding the more personal subjects. It isn't until our meal is complete that Ricky brings up tomorrow night's dinner.

"If you tell me your address, I can pick you up for the dinner."

"Where is the dinner?"

"Hotel Carmichael." He grins. "Walkable from here."

"Fancy."

"Really? How fancy?"

I eye him up and down. "Dark-suit-fancy." My thoughts go between the idea of Ricky in a tailored suit and wondering what I will wear. "I wasn't expecting such a nice venue. Hotel Carmichael has only been open a few years."

Ricky suddenly looks concerned. "I have one suit."

"The partners are old-school. Change up the shirt and tie, and the suit won't matter."

He inhales, his nostrils flaring. "I'm feeling like tomorrow's dinner is an interview."

"Essentially, it is."

He shrugs. "Even if I don't get the job, I've had a good time tonight." His lips curl upward. "What you said about the world beyond Riverbend being lonely, it is. And I have a roommate. Tonight was great, talking to someone and not having to pretend to be someone else."

A roommate?

Is Ricky in a relationship?

Why ask me to this dinner?

"A roommate? Why not take her to the dinner?"

Ricky laughs. "Because she is a he." He lifts his hands. "Always has been, to my knowledge. And in a nutshell, Max is the opposite of stable."

I let out a breath, thankful he isn't living with a woman, while also chastising myself for caring. "Ricky, tomorrow, don't pretend to be anyone else. You've worked hard enough to be invited to this dinner. That doesn't happen to everyone. The partners already see something in you. Just be you." A smile lifts my cheeks. "I'm not sure I can refer to you as Rich or Richard."

He reaches out, lifting his hand palm up on the table. "We've known each other for a long time and have been dating off and on." He meets my gaze.

The din of diners around us disappears as I slowly lift my hand and place it in his. The warmth of his touch envelops me as he wraps his fingers around mine. When I look back up, he's still staring at me.

"We're on again," he says, his deep voice rumbling like thunder, warning of an approaching storm. "I can't thank you enough."

Retrieving my hand, I inhale and sit taller. "This was nice, talking to someone. I hope you get the job you want, but remember what you said—no strings. As soon as tomorrow's dinner is over, we're off again."

He nods as his Adam's apple bobs. "No strings."

"If you give me your phone, I'll add my number and address." I wink. "Probably something a boyfriend would know."

"Good idea. Give me yours, and I'll do the same."

We exchange phones. As I enter my name into his contacts, I see it's already there, listed as *Marilyn J. Do not answer*. My blood boils. "It seems you have my number."

He looks up at me with large eyes. "Oh, I forgot. I've had it for a long time. I don't have your address."

My hands start to shake as I enter my address in the contact information. Emotions I'd tempered begin to build. He's had my number and never used it. Not only that, but he had a reminder not to answer. I add my address but leave his note intact.

As we again exchange phones, Ricky says, "I didn't know if you had a new number. That one has been in there for a while."

"Like seven years?"

His countenance changes. "We've established I'm an ass, or I was. Can we move beyond that?"

Can we?

"Sure," I say curtly. "The reminder is good. You're

an ass. I'm an angel for helping you out, and soon, we'll be off again, like we've been for seven years."

"Marilyn, stop. Tonight was nice. Let's play on that."

Pressing my lips together, I watch as the waiter lays the black folder on the table. "What time should I expect you?"

"Cocktails are at six thirty." He tilts his head as he opens the folder. "I can pick you up at six."

Clenching my teeth, I watch as he places his credit card in the folder. Once it's closed, I push my chair back and stand. "Thank you for dinner. I need to go."

"I can walk you out to your car." He stands and looks down at the folder, obviously torn about what to do.

"No worries, *Richard*. I can walk myself to my car." Just like I've been doing for the last seven years.

I don't say the last part. Instead, I lift my coat and purse from the back of the chair and turn away before he can see the tears teetering on my eyelids.

By the time I reach my car, the salty traitors have glided down my cheeks, followed by more. My temples ache from my swift shift in emotions. I don't even notice the cold until I press the button, start the car, and the heat radiates from the vents.

Ricky had my number.

It would be better if he didn't—but he does.

He's just never called it.

"This was a bad idea," I say aloud. "Get your shit together, Marilyn. One more evening. Play nice and never speak to him again."

Chapter Nine

Ricky

F*uck.*

It isn't until I'm waiting for the waiter to bring back my credit card that I look at what Marilyn entered. As soon as the screen is visible, I feel the fucking floor drop out from under me.

Shit.

Clenching my teeth, I look toward the front of the restaurant, hoping I can catch her, but I know she's gone. Not only didn't I remember that Marilyn's number was in my phone, but I sure as hell forgot that I had *do not answer* as part of her name. As soon as I reach my vehicle, I hit the name of my best friend in my contacts. Getting inside the car, I slam the door shut. Justin answers on the first ring.

"Are you injured? Why are you calling?"

"Fuck, I'm not sure what to do. Is Devan there?"

"You could call her number if you want to talk to her," he says.

I pound the back of my hand against the steering wheel and stare out the windshield at the people walking along the sidewalk in the brisk, chilled air. "I want to talk to you, without my sister's input, or, fuck...knowledge."

Justin's voice drops in volume. "She's upstairs in her office, grading papers. What the hell did you do?"

"Now, or years ago?" I ask, feeling guiltier than I have since Marilyn and I parted ways after the graduation party. I can't get the look she gave me out of my mind, the one after seeing my note in my contacts. No wonder she left so fast.

"Rick, what's happened?"

"Do you have a few minutes? This isn't a quick story, and I'd rather be talking in person over a few beers."

"I have the time," my best friend says. "I'm not driving to Indy."

"I wasn't expecting that. Remember how impressed I was that Marilyn had an internship at the firm Parker and Stevens?"

"Marilyn James, Devan's best friend?"

"Yes, that Marilyn. How many do you know?"

"It's an old name, but she's the only one."

"That firm," I say, going on, "is a well-respected wealth management company with a Carmel office."

"Oh, now I remember. Devan said you called the other day to ask if she still worked there."

"And she does. I've been interviewing at the same firm. The other day, I got an invitation to a dinner with the partners, and it asked for a plus-one. I thought that by working there, Marilyn could help me with the interview process. I thought she could be my plus-one."

"I thought the two of you hated each other, or was that some kind of act?"

"That's kind of where this story begins. Around the time of Devan's graduation, I may have mentioned I hooked up with someone. It wasn't a big deal, and I didn't say who..."

"No fucking way." Justin's voice is no longer soft. "You and Marilyn? Devan said you kissed."

"It was more than that. After...well, I didn't want a relationship, and fuck, she was so young. I had no way of knowing I was her first, until it was obvious."

"Oh man. Shit. No wonder she despises you."

"It wasn't like I pledged my undying love. It was a hookup. No strings. And then over the years, I found her animosity fun...a little. Mostly, being the asshole that I am, I avoided her. Then with you and Devan, we agreed to play nice for you. I even apologized during your reception."

"And now?"

My view through the windows is muted by condensation. I close my eyes, picturing Marilyn looking at my phone, seeing her number and the note I'd put there seven fucking years ago. "Now, I think I fucked up again."

"You didn't sleep with her *again*?" Justin emphasizes the last word.

"No. I didn't. I want to, but that's not the fuckup."

"Whoa, you want to?"

"We had dinner together tonight." I rub my fingertips over my chin. "She's grown up. In all the right places. And it was good to talk to someone who knows the things, places, and people I know. Tonight was supposed to be a trial run for tomorrow night's partner dinner. She agreed to be my plus-one. We came up with a story that we've been off-and-on-again dating for years."

"How did you fuck up?"

"Marilyn asked for my phone to put her number and address into my contacts. When she did, she saw her name."

"You already had her number?"

"I'd totally forgotten that it was there. When I

called her to ask if she'd be my plus-one, I called her office number, one I found online. That's not all." I take a deep breath. "Seven years ago, when I put her number in my contacts, I added a note."

"Shit. What did it say?"

"Do not answer."

"Dude, you either need to cancel tomorrow night's dinner or do something drastic. I love you like a brother, but you're an asshole—not only for years ago, but for today. You can't expect her to play your fake-date after that."

I know he's right. That doesn't make what he's saying any easier to hear.

The clock on the dashboard tells me that it's after nine.

An idea comes to me. "She gave me her address. Do you think if I apologize in person…? Fuck, I'd forgotten all about that note."

"She could slam the door in your face."

"What would Devan do?"

"If I really pissed her off, she would tell me."

"And what would you do?"

"Anything and everything I could to make it right."

"I'm going to stop at a store and get flowers. I need to make this right."

"I have a question," Justin says. "Why are you making it right?"

"Because I hurt her. Fuck, I saw the way her expression changed, but I didn't realize until after she was gone what she saw."

"Or are you making it right so she'll still go with you to the dinner?"

"I mean...yes, but..." I let out a long breath. "I didn't mean to hurt her."

"Tonight, or seven years ago?"

"Seven years ago, I didn't realize I hurt her. Some women are fine with hooking up, no strings. Marilyn never said she wanted more."

"How could she? You had a reminder not to answer her calls."

I clear my throat. "Fuck the dinner. I'm going to apologize. And one more thing, don't tell Devan."

"I don't lie to my wife."

"Omission isn't lying. Marilyn said she never told Devan. If you tell her, she'll be upset with Marilyn, and that's not what either of them needs."

"Fuck," Justin growls. "Work this out, not only for Devan, but for the two of you."

"Thanks." I disconnect the call as my shame and guilt multiply.

How many phones have I had over the last seven years?

Why the hell would all of that contact information transfer?

Before I can talk myself out of it, I set my GPS to Marilyn's address. I start thinking about what I can take as a peace offering. All the local florists are closed, but the supermarkets usually have flowers. And then, the idea hits me.

Chapter Ten

Marilyn

"Do not answer."

I can't get the note out of my head. I shouldn't have answered his call to my office. I sure as hell shouldn't have agreed to help him. Standing in front of my closet, I'm contemplating canceling tomorrow night's dinner. Why should I care if he gets a job at Parker and Stevens? The longer I stare at my small stash of cocktail dresses, the more appealing the idea of canceling is to me. After all, if he gets the job, I'll see him more often. Going to one dinner was about as masochistic as I get. Daily interactions would be too much.

Closing the closet door, I settle on my decision.

No cocktail dress.

No formal dinner at the Hotel Carmichael.

No more Ricky Dunn—ever.

The simple decision eases some of the throbbing in my temples.

In the bathroom, I turn on the water in my bathtub. The tub is one of my favorite features in my apartment. It's deep, with claw feet, and perfect for soaking. At the vanity, I wash away the day's makeup, noticing the puffiness around my eyes.

"No more," I say to my reflection. "Never again."

My reflection agrees, giving me a sturdy smile in response. Grabbing a hair tie, I secure my long hair on top of my head in a messy bun. Next, in the kitchen, I find a half-finished bottle of Moscato near the back of my refrigerator and pour a healthy glass.

Back in the bathroom, the air is warm and heavy with humidity from the hot water filling the tub. Setting the glass down on the table near the tub, I begin to shed my clothes. The boots came off as soon as I entered the door of my apartment. Now, the blouse, slacks, and my bra are littering the bathroom floor. I'm about to push down my underwear when the buzzer rings. It's the buzzer for the intercom from the ground floor.

My thoughts immediately go to deliveries. While I contemplated a pity order to Uber Eats, I didn't do it. Is there something I'm forgetting? If there is, I don't want the delivery man to leave it on the stoop all night.

I turn off the running water, grab my robe from the hook, and tie the sash as I tread toward the front door and the intercom. “Hello?” I say into the box on the wall.

“Can I come up?”

I jump away from the box, startled by the voice coming through the speaker. Bravely moving forward, I press the button. “No. And you saved me a text message. I’m unable to attend the partner dinner tomorrow night. Don’t call. I won’t answer.”

“Marilyn, please?”

“Goodbye, Ricky. Good luck with whatever life has for you.”

“I brought you something.”

Shaking my head, I straighten my neck. “Leave it or take it. I don’t care.”

“It’s cold out here, but it could still melt.”

Melt?

Ricky speaks next. “I found caramel ice cream at Graeter’s. Thankfully, they’re open late.”

New tears prick my eyes. “Go to the dinner alone. Be honest with the partners.”

“I don’t care about the dinner. Please let me up. It’s freezing out here, especially holding a pint of ice cream.”

In place of answering, I push the button to unlock the main door. It's at that moment that I realize I'm wearing a short satin robe that barely covers my ass. My boobs are free and not truly restrained by the small robe. And that doesn't even take into account my messy bun and makeup-free face.

Well, fuck him.

Less than a minute later, there's a knock on my door. A quick peek through the peephole confirms who is outside. From this view, I can't tell if he really has caramel ice cream, but if he does, that's great. I'll eat it with my wine in the bathtub.

Unlocking the dead bolt, I pull open the door a few inches. My first instinct is to look for the ice cream. The pint is there in his bare hands. His coat is unzipped, and he's still filling out the jeans and button-down shirt as well as he did earlier at the restaurant. The only thing missing from before is his smile.

"May I please come in?"

Keeping the door from opening farther with my foot, I extend my hand. "I'll take the ice cream, and you can leave."

With a forced grin, Ricky holds the pint out of my reach. His chocolate eyes scan from my bare feet to my messy bun, and his smile grows. "Damn, you're hot."

Taking a step back, I push the door closed. In the

millisecond it took for me to move, Ricky has wedged his shoe between the door and the doorjamb.

"Marilyn, please let me explain."

"Fine," I say, releasing the door. "Explain and leave. I'm still not going to the partners' dinner." My instinct is to wrap my arms around my midsection to secure the robe.

Ricky steps into my apartment, his eyes wide as he looks all around the living room. "Whoa, this is a nice apartment." He turns to meet my gaze. "You can shut the door, Marilyn. I won't do anything stupid. I think I've already covered that base."

I close the door but stand near it with my arms now crossed over my breasts and my lips pressed together. "Hurry," I say. "I have a date waiting."

It's with my tub, wine, and now the ice cream, but he doesn't need to know that.

"Is that how you dress for your date?"

"No. I plan to be completely nude for the date, not that it's any of your business."

Ricky comes forward and hands me the ice cream. "It's caramel macchiato. They didn't have plain caramel. I'm sure it's not as good as your grandma's..."

I take the pint.

"I've never tried Graeter's."

He pushes his hands into the pockets of his jacket.

"It has milk chocolate caramel truffles and Heath toffee pieces."

"I don't have any food allergies, but thanks for the ingredient list."

Ricky's cheeks rise. "There's the smart mouth I'm used to."

"Don't be." I motion between us. "There's nothing to get used to between me and you."

"I want you to believe me. I didn't remember that I had your number." When I don't respond, he continues. "I sure as hell didn't recall that note. If I did, would I have handed my phone off to you?"

"I don't give a damn about the note. Here's the news flash. You won't need to answer, because I won't be calling."

Ricky nods. "I get it. And fuck the partners' dinner. I meant what I said earlier in the evening. I had a great time with you. Don't make that stupid note from years ago into something more than what it is."

I lift my eyebrows. "What it is? It's obviously your reminder to blow me off. Well, I never called you, Ricky. I never asked you for one damn thing. It was obvious that I meant nothing to you."

"We said no strings. I didn't lie to you."

The ice cream is now sitting on a small table by my couch, and my arms are again crossed over my breasts. "Right," I say with too much glee. "You didn't lie to me. I didn't call you. Everything is perfect."

Ricky takes a step back, turns a circle, and faces me. "Nothing is perfect. I don't care about the dinner tomorrow night. I don't want you to be upset."

"My mood has no bearing on you. Just leave. Try not to be an ass tomorrow night, and the dinner should go well." I let my arms fall to my sides. "Please leave. My bath is getting cold."

"Is that your date?"

"As a matter of fact, it is—a bath, a glass of wine, and now I have ice cream. I know how to have a good time."

"I'd like to join you."

My eyebrows shoot upward. "Oh, hell no. That's not happening."

He takes a step toward me. "I could show you how sorry I am."

I refuse to acknowledge the way my nipples are hardening and my core is tightening, as I continue to stare him down. "Goodbye, Ricky Dunn, Rich, Richard, Dick, or whatever you're calling yourself."

He nods once. "Maybe after your date, you can consider forgiving me."

Walking to the door, I open it. "Feel free to delete my contact information. I'll delete yours."

He stops inches away. "I'm not deleting your information." His eyes sweep from my lips back to my eyes. "It's taking every ounce of control not to kiss you right now."

I shake my head.

"I'm not lying, Marilyn. I never have lied to you. I think life turned out the way we both wanted, the dreams we didn't even know we had seven years ago. I didn't know I wanted out of farming. You didn't know you'd accomplish so much. I didn't know that while I wasn't watching, you became someone I find irresistible. Whether you're smart-mouthing me or, one day, kissing me, I never knew you would be part of my dream."

Swallowing, I step back. His shoulder brushes mine as he turns to leave.

As soon as he's across the threshold, I close the door.

For a moment or two, I wait to see if he knocks. When he doesn't, I walk away, taking the ice cream to the kitchen, grabbing a spoon, and making my way back to my bathtub.

Chapter Eleven

Ricky

When I wake the next morning, I hear sounds of life beyond my bedroom door. Reaching for my phone, I see multiple text messages from Justin, one from Devan, and no text or call from Marilyn. Of course she didn't contact me. She said she wouldn't. That doesn't mean I'm not disappointed.

Curiosity takes me to my sister's text first—the time stamp tells me it was sent earlier this morning.

"What the hell, Ricky? Seven years ago! Marilyn deserves better. Don't be mad at Justin. We don't keep

secrets from each other. Maybe you should try that. Make this right."

"Fuck," I growl and roll to my back in my bed. Sunlight streams from around the cheap mini blinds on my window, telling me that it's past time to wake up. Tonight's the night of the partner dinner, and even though I RSVP'd for two, I'm going solo.

Great. Not only am I alone, but I'm also not even stable enough to RSVP as one. I flop my arm over my eyes, remembering Marilyn's expression as she stared down at my phone. If I could turn back time, I wouldn't go back to seven years ago. I would go back to yesterday and erase that note or, maybe, erase her number altogether, allowing her to enter it.

I reread my sister's text message—try honesty. I did that last night and all it got me was Marilyn's wrath and out nine bucks for a pint of caramel ice cream. I begin reading Justin's texts. The first few are from last night, asking what I did to make up to Marilyn and asking how it went.

"Shitty. That's how it went."

The last one is from this morning, confessing he told Devan my story. Not only my story, but our story —Marilyn's and mine. Shit, now we're an our. That wouldn't be so bad. My lips curl as I recall the way she looked last night at her apartment, that sexy short robe, her hair all piled on top of her head. She was fucking gorgeous.

The thoughts I had after our hookup seem ridiculous today. I worried about her age, because seven years ago, she was only eighteen. It's not that twenty-five is old; there's still a ten-year difference between us. It's that ten years doesn't feel as large anymore.

The last sentence of Devan's text message repeats in my thoughts: Make this right.

I don't know if I can, but I know without a doubt that I want to. I want to make things right. Throwing on a pair of nylon shorts, I make my way out of the bedroom. After a stop in the bathroom, I head toward the kitchen, stopping in the doorway.

There's a woman, with hair the color of Marilyn's, sitting at the breakfast bar, facing the other direction and looking down at a phone. One of her slender shoulders is exposed, revealing part of a colorful tattoo.

Does Marilyn have a tattoo?

For a split second, I think it's her, here, in my apartment. If she's here, she hasn't been with me. My hands ball into fists at my sides, thinking of Marilyn with Max.

I clear my throat as a warning.

The woman turns. "Hey. Max said it was okay if I hang out for a while."

She isn't Marilyn.

In that second, I realize she doesn't hold a candle to Marilyn. This woman isn't ugly, but she doesn't have Marilyn's blue eyes, turned-up nose, cheekbones, or soft lips. "Sure. Make yourself at home. I'm Rich, by the way."

She grins. "Then why do you live in this crappy apartment?"

"Name is Rich, as in short for Richard, because if I were actually rich, you're right, I wouldn't live here." And I wouldn't have a roommate who brings home different women every night.

"I'm Kyla," she says, extending her hand.

We shake. "Nice to meet you."

"Yeah, there's a problem at my apartment, and Max said he could make room for me."

My eyes open wide. "Are you and Max serious? Like, in a relationship?"

Her smile grows. "Oh yes. Very serious."

Inwardly, I grimace, knowing Max is not serious with any woman. "Okay, so are you moving in?"

"Not permanently."

I rub my hand over my prickly chin and wonder what the hell is happening. Could Max be serious about one woman, or is she just a glitch—a delay—in his revolving door? Either way, if we're now a household of three, I shouldn't have to pay half the rent.

Instead of bringing that up with Kyla, I pour myself a cup of coffee.

"I made muffins," Kyla says. "There are a few in the microwave."

"You made them?"

"From a box, but yeah."

Opening the microwave door, I see the fresh muffins as the scent of sugar and blueberries fills my senses. Maybe Kyla won't make too bad of a roommate. Peeling back the paper, I take a big bite, the blueberries melting in my mouth. "That's fucking delicious."

"Figure I should do something if I'm staying here."

When it comes to questions about women, my go-to is Devan. Currently, my sister is teaching seventh graders about science, so I decide to ask the woman who happens to be sitting in my kitchen in an oversized shirt and tight exercise shorts.

"Kyla, can I ask you something?"

She looks up from her phone. "I'm in your kitchen."

"You are. I kind of fucked up with a woman last night."

She tilts her head and widens her eyes. "Kind of...?"

"Okay, I fucked up. How do I make it right?"

"Are you going to tell me what you did?"

I consider her question for a moment. "No, it's a long story. Let's just say that I've known her for a long time. We come from the same hometown. She's been friends with my little sister forever. Last night, I hurt her without meaning to. I'd do anything to take it back. I can't, because she doesn't want to talk to me."

Pouting her lips, Kyla nods. "She doesn't want to *talk* to you, then communicate some other way. This is the future." She lifts her phone. "I can talk on this or text. There's email and still the rarely seen, some would argue more sentimental, handwritten messages. Smoke signals are a little impractical, but I'm sure there's some mode of communication you can figure out."

"If I do any of those options, how will I know if she even reads it? What if she doesn't?"

"Then you're no worse off than you are now."

I reach for a second muffin. "I tried last night. I took a pint of her favorite ice cream to her apartment."

Kyla sits taller, stretching her neck. "Ice cream is good. I'm guessing that didn't work?"

I shake my head.

"Maybe she needs time. You know, a warm bath and a good night's sleep."

That makes me grin. "She said she had a date with a bath."

"Yeah, you fucked up, because when a woman turns to her tub, she's pissed off."

"What can I do?"

"I guess you have two options."

"Two options for what?" Max asks as he steps into the kitchen. His hair is wet, and he's wearing black pants and a shirt with the shoe store's moniker on his chest.

"Rich pissed off his girlfriend," Kyla says.

"Wait." My roommate stops and lifts his arms. "Since when do you have a girlfriend?"

"She's not my girlfriend. She's a girl and a friend."

"Does she know that she's not a girlfriend?" Kyla asks.

"Yes. I mean, she does. We've never put labels on things. No strings."

Kyla looks at Max, and they both nod knowingly.

"What?" I ask, ready to take the rest of my coffee and muffin back to the safety and serenity of my room.

Kyla hops down from the stool, goes to Max, pushes up on her tiptoes, and, lifting her hand, ruffles Max's wet curls. "Thanks for a place to stay."

His expression when he looks down at her is somehow different from any expression I've ever before witnessed. "Anytime."

Maybe there is something between these two.

When Kyla turns back to me, she has one fist on her hip. "Let me share a secret with you, Rich. A woman doesn't soak in a long, hot bath over a *friend*."

She shakes her head. "Nope. It doesn't happen. Maybe the real issue is that she wants more than you want."

"I'm one hundred percent certain that isn't true. She wants nothing to do with me."

"Listen, I'm not saying that she's lying to you. I'm saying that she's probably trying to convince both you and her that she wants nothing to do with you."

I'm wondering if a woman I just met in my kitchen is really that insightful about someone she's never met. "How do you know this, other than being a woman?"

"Being a woman is in itself a criterion."

Max grins. "I'm not sure who you think Kyla is." Before I can answer without upsetting everyone, he goes on. "Her professional title is Doctor Kyla." He grins. "Dr. Brenner."

"As in your last name?" I ask.

"I'm his sister, and when I'm not staying at my brother's apartment, I work as a psychotherapist. My specialty is relationship counseling."

"Well, shit," I stutter. "You're a real doctor?"

"I have a PhD, so yes, a real doctor. I can't heal your broken arm, but I can help with broken hearts. By the way, that session will be $300. I'll have my receptionist bill you."

With my lips together, I move my eyes between Max and Kyla, wondering if she's serious, and also, how one sibling can have her doctorate while the other is a professional mall worker.

"I'm teasing about the bill," Kyla says, making me smile.

"How the hell are you two siblings?"

Max goes to the microwave and takes the last muffin. "I know. It's uncanny. What can I say? I'm fortunate to have the happy-go-lucky genes. Kyla got stuck with our dad's overachieving DNA."

I turn to Kyla. "Dr. Brenner, where is the line between trying to make it right and stalking? Right now, I want to go to her workplace with a dozen roses and beg for forgiveness."

"Does she mean that much to you? You said she's your sister's friend and your friend...that's all."

Leaning against the kitchen counter, I take another drink of my coffee. "I think I want her to mean more. If she'll give me another chance."

Kyla winks. "Work on communication. The rest will come."

Chapter Twelve

Marilyn

It's difficult to concentrate on my clients' financial profiles when my thoughts continually circle back to Ricky and his interview dinner tonight. I must be a masochist because when I woke this morning, I was more worried about him at the dinner than I was about my own feelings. Last night, it was the exact opposite. The sense of rejection was heavier than it had been seven years ago.

That long ago, I didn't know what to feel. I'd agreed to our terms. I was upset Ricky had stuck to them, which, in hindsight, wasn't fair to him. Last night was different. While he'd given the same no-strings speech, last night was about helping a friend, a friend I've never gotten over. The entire evening, from our drinks at the bar to our dinner, was enjoyable, more so than I expected. Not a minute with Ricky was boring. No discussion of languages or countries visited.

Somewhere in my inner teenage self, I imagined a path forward.

It isn't like I'm looking for the love of my life. It's that after years of navigating the world basically on my own, I saw the possibility of a partner. Ricky could be a partner who understands my day-to-day work and enjoys the comfort of our shared friends and family.

Finding that note on his phone was exponentially more upsetting than the fact that he never called or texted me after our one night—the one night without strings. That note next to my name meant that he not only didn't plan to call me, but he didn't want to answer if I called.

"Ms. James," Klara says as she pushes my office door inward. "You have a delivery."

I tear my eyes away from my computer screens. "A delivery?"

She comes into my office holding an envelope.

"Why not have the mail person deliver it?" I ask as I take it from her. The paper is thick and soft beneath my fingertips. There's no address or stamp, just my name written in flowing cursive. I look up at our receptionist. "Did someone hand-deliver this?"

"Yes, ma'am. A man. He didn't give his name, only asked if you were here and if I could take this to you."

"Should we have it tested for anthrax?" I ask with a grin.

She lifts her hands. "I hope not." Her smile returns. "He seemed nice enough. Handsome, too."

"Thank you, Klara."

"I think you have an admirer."

"If I do, it will be the best thing to happen in a long time."

Klara closes the office door on her way out, leaving me staring down at the envelope. Assuming it isn't poisonous, I should probably open it. As I reach for my letter opener, a rarely used office tool, my cell phone vibrates, and I see Devan's name on the screen. A quick look at the clock tells me that school is probably out for the weekend.

"Hey," I say as I answer.

"I'm mad at you."

"You are?" I ask, leaning forward, suddenly worried why one of my best friends would be mad at me, but knowing the answer in the pit of my stomach. "Devan, you can't be mad. You're one of my best friends."

"Am I?"

"You know you are."

"Do we tell each other everything?" she asks.

Shit.

"We tell each other *almost* everything."

"Marilyn, I've shared everything with you. You told me your first sex was with a guy at Ball State. You said he was handsome and smooth-talking and you never wanted to see him again. I believed you."

"I never technically said he was at Ball State. You used context clues to assume that part."

"Handsome and smooth-talking...Ricky?" Her voice goes higher as she says her brother's name.

"Okay, that part was a lie." It wasn't when I said it. "Your brother is a total ass, and I'm sorry, Dev, but I'm not even going to play nice for you and Justin anymore. I hope I never see him as long as I live."

"Oh my God!" she screams. "You like him. You really like him."

Is she even listening?

"No, Devan. The opposite."

"No. I know you. I lived with you for four years. If you don't like someone, you forget they exist. Remember that guy from your calculus class our freshman year? You simply pretended to no longer share the same air. And then there was the guy our junior year you met in swimming class."

"What an asinine class for college students."

"Yeah," she goes on, "but you really liked him.

When he turned into a jerk, you swore you hated him. That's what you do when you like someone."

"I love you, Dev. Stick to teaching. Psychology isn't your forte."

"Justin told me what happened—what happened last night." Her voice is quieter and pathetically appeasing.

"I'm fine. It was a good reminder of what a total jackass your brother is. I won't forget it again."

"You aren't fine. Come down here for the weekend. Jill will be here for her niece's birthday."

I'd forgotten Jill telling me about that. "I don't think going back to my childhood bedroom will make this better."

"Then stay with us. We have extra rooms. I'll have Jill come over, and the three of us can come clean about all the things we haven't told one another."

"I think that's the only one, for me." I swallow. "I'm sorry, Dev. He's your brother. I was... Well, afterward, I was ashamed and embarrassed. He still thought of me as a kid, and honestly, when he realized he was my first, he freaked out."

"Gosh, sounds absolutely orgasmic."

A laugh comes from my throat. "It wasn't. I bet he'd be a lot better now." What did I just say? "Nope. That wasn't me talking. Someone must have cut into our call."

"Think about it. Justin and I would love to show you the things we've done with the house. We can sit by the fire and drink spiked cider."

"With cinnamon?" I ask.

"Of course."

"You're not mad at me?"

"I am," she says. "But now that you know I am, I can get over it. Mostly, I want to give you a hug and tell you that I love you."

Tears sting my eyes. "I could use a hug."

Driving to Riverbend would be better than sitting in my apartment, wondering about Ricky's dinner and feeling guilty for not following through on my promise to help him. Those thoughts remind me of the letter in front of me.

Tucking my phone between my cheek and shoulder, I open the envelope, remove the page, and unfold it. My gaze goes to the bottom of the paper. Signed—Ricky.

"Dev, I'll call you back and let you know my decision. I have another few hours here at work."

"Okay, I'm going to stop at the grocery store and stock up on the best drinks and snacks for girl time."

"What about Justin?"

"He can be our sexy waiter."

Another laugh. "Um, if you say so."

"Call back after work."

"I will." We disconnect our call. I lay my phone on my desk and smooth out the page, reading the flowing words.

Dear Marilyn,

Someone told me that handwritten letters are a rarely used form of communication. I read where they are also the sincerest. It's easy and fast to send a text message. An email takes only seconds longer. A hand-written note takes time, penmanship, and patience. That doesn't even take into account the delivery.

I didn't want to wait on the USPS, so I delivered this letter personally to your office.

If you haven't stopped reading yet, I might have a chance of you reading to the very end. I told you last night that I was sorry. That's an insignificant explanation of a complex emotion. I'm not sure the English language has a word capable of expressing my distress over causing you pain.

Hurting you wasn't my intention—neither years ago nor last night.

The partners' dinner means nothing if I can't consider you a friend—or more. You see, working at Parker and Stevens would mean more to me if I knew I could see your beautiful smile, hear your glorious laugh-

ter, and bask in your presence. Without those qualities, the firm would mean nothing more than any other.

I hope you continued reading, and I hope that when I call, you will answer. If you call, I will always answer.

Yours,

Ricky

I read the letter to the end.

Yours.

Yours?

What the actual hell?

Despite my gut reaction to his sign-off, I'm ashamed to say I read the handwritten note multiple times before folding it neatly and placing it back in the envelope. To be honest, I'm not sure what I'm thinking.

A look up at my screen, and I admit that the wealth perspectives and investment growth of my clients is far away from my current radar. I'm about to call it a day when there's a knock on my office door.

Not waiting for a command from me, the door opens. While I expect to see Klara with another message, a letter or maybe more ice cream, instead, I'm met with the green stare of Bryce Perkins. My ex.

"Marilyn, can I ask you for a favor?"

I grit my teeth. "No, Bryce. It's Friday, and I have plans."

He comes toward my desk, wearing his business casual, pants, a sweater, and a suit coat. The aroma of his cologne proceeds him as he nears. There's no question that Bryce is a handsome man. The truth of the matter is that, like T.J., the guy from the gym, Bryce is boring and too self-assured for his own good.

"I know it's late notice," he says, "but I'm supposed to attend the dinner tonight for the applicants for our new entry-level position."

I sit taller and purse my lips. "Are you inviting me? It is a little late." I look at my watch. "There's only two hours to cocktails."

His expression pinches. "How do you know about it?"

"A friend told me."

"Are you available?" he asks hopefully.

Standing, I meet his gaze. "No, Bryce. I'm not available at the last minute to be your plus-one. What happened? Does your current flavor of the month have a broken nail?"

"Beth and I have been dating for two months. She's coming down with something, and she suggested I ask you."

"Why would she do that?"

"Because she knows we're over as a couple. You know, you're not a threat."

I can't help but laugh. "That has to be one of the worst pickup lines ever. I'm not sure why everyone thinks I'm the one to help with favors, but news flash, I'm not. I can't possibly go with you to the dinner. I'm already attending with one of the applicants."

"You are?"

I wasn't a few minutes ago, but after being told I'm not a threat, hell yes. "I am, and I need to get ready—you know, in a nonthreatening way. See you tonight, Bryce."

As he walks away, I sit back in my chair, enjoying the energy flowing through my circulation. Turning Bryce down is just the kick I need. And being told I'm not a threat is the incentive I needed to stop feeling sorry for myself.

I can be a threat.

When it comes to Bryce, I'm not interested enough not to be a threat.

Quickly, I send Devan a text message.

"I've had a change of plans. I'll drive down to Riverbend on Saturday. See you then."

. . .

Now, I need to hurry.

Chapter Thirteen

Ricky

I remind myself that working for Parker and Stevens has been my goal for years. When I learned Marilyn had an internship there, I was damn impressed. I'd already done my research and knew what a prestigious firm it was. Making it down to the final group of applicants for…they haven't told us… however many positions, is an accomplishment.

Then why, as I stand in front of the bathroom mirror, feeling the stiffness of the new shirt and working to create the perfect knot in the new tie, aren't I excited about my opportunity?

Kyla stands in the open doorway. "You look good, Rich."

"Do you want to go to a dinner with me?"

She looks down at the tight pants and blouse she's wearing—professional from the waist up for her tele-visits with her patients. "I'm afraid I'd need more notice. And I'm even more certain that I'm not your first choice."

"Seeing as I only met you this morning…" I don't finish the sentence.

"My landlord said the water heater should be fixed by Monday. I'll be out of your way after that."

Exhaling, I smooth the tie and button one button of my suit coat. "You're not in my way. Max is the one with the revolving door." I turn to Kyla with wide eyes. "Sorry if you're not supposed to know that."

She laughs. "I know that. It's why I brought my own sheets for his bed."

Since Max is at work, Kyla and I are alone in the apartment. To be honest, it's less weird to be with his sister than with one of his many girlfriends. "How did you two turn out so different?"

She crosses her arms over her chest and leans against the doorjamb. "Do you want the sister's answer or the psychotherapist's answer?"

"Are they different?"

"Of course. A sister sees things through a particular lens. Max is my little brother. Do I wish he had my drive? I do. We've been different since we were kids. When we were very young, he followed me everywhere

I went. As we grew up, he started finding his own way. Our parents were pretty hands-off. When they finally started to notice him, they couldn't understand why he didn't strive for more."

"He's content," I say. "Sometimes too content."

Kyla laughs. "As a therapist, strictly from observation, because Max doesn't want to be psychoanalyzed, I think he watched me work my ass off with little to no recognition from our parents and decided it wasn't worth the effort. They noticed him more when he screwed up."

"What about you?"

"I didn't accomplish what I have for anyone except myself. I'm happy with where I am and what I do. The hard work paid off. The thing is, Max is happy with where he is and what he does. What about you?"

I think about the answer. "I think I want a job, something to make all the work of going back to college worth it. I'm not sorry I chose to go back. Maybe I'm sorry I didn't do it sooner, but then again, I didn't hate farming."

Kyla's eyes widen. "I didn't know you farmed."

My smile widens. "I didn't know Max had a sister."

"There's nothing wrong with going solo to a dinner. I do it all the time. That's where Max and I differ. I'm comfortable being alone. He seeks companionship."

"He gets it—a lot." I nod, silently asking for a clear path from the bathroom.

Kyla steps back.

Making my way to my room, with the door open as I throw a few last-minute items into a backpack, I say, "I don't want Max to sleep in my room, but I've decided to take a friend up on an invitation. After the dinner, I'm heading down to Riverbend for the week-end. You can sleep in here, in case Max comes home with a friend."

"Are you serious?"

"You'll probably want to use your own sheets."

"Thank you. I'll have it clean and ready for you by Sunday night. Show the people at this dinner that you are confident without a plus-one."

"Thanks, Dr. Brenner. I suppose I should take your advice."

Opening the door to the apartment, I'm met with a beautiful blue gaze, one I never expected to see. Words fail me as I take in Marilyn, from her hair twisted behind her head, to her mesmerizing eyes, turned-up nose, red lips drawn into a bow, to lower. The long coat she's wearing is unbuttoned, giving me a peek at the black dress beneath. The neckline scoops just enough to catch a glimpse of the round globes of her breasts. The dress tapers at her waist, showcasing her curves, the material ends at her mid-calves, and she's wearing high black heels.

I finally manage to articulate my sentiment. "I can't believe you're here."

"I don't bail on a friend, even if I never want to see him again."

"You look amazing."

"Rich."

Marilyn's eyes open wide, and her expression hardens. I turn to see Kyla standing behind me, holding my backpack. "You forgot this…" She stares at Marilyn.

"Forget it," Marilyn says with a shake of her head. "I'm an idiot."

I reach for Marilyn's hand, not allowing her to bolt. "Stop. She's not—"

"I suppose this is Max?"

Kyla's smile grows. "I'm Max's sister." She looks at me and back to Marilyn. "Are you the woman Rich upset?"

"It's hard to know if I'm the only," Marilyn responds. "He could have a long list."

Regaining my ability to speak, I begin introductions. "Marilyn, this is Kyla. As she said, she's Max's sister. Kyla, this is Marilyn, the woman I mentioned."

"He more than mentioned you," Kyla says. "I'm glad you changed your mind." She tilts her head toward me. "This guy has it bad for you."

"We're just friends," Marilyn says dismissively, before adding, "It's nice to meet you, Kyla."

"You two play nice at the dinner," Kyla says, nudging me forward and closing the door behind me.

I meet Marilyn's gaze. "I don't know what to say. I thought I'd blown everything."

"You did."

"You're giving me another chance?"

"I realized if I didn't show, I would be the one who didn't follow through. For the record, I don't want to be the reason you don't follow through on your dream."

"Thank you," I say sincerely.

"Also, I Ubered here."

"Good." Offering her my arm, I go on. "I'll drive. I like the idea of you in my car."

At the sight of my arm, Marilyn narrows her eyes.

"If we're dating, we should probably touch."

"No strings." She lays her hand in the crook of my arm. "There is something I need to warn you about. I learned today that my ex will be at the dinner."

"Your ex?"

Together, we walk down the hallway to the outside door. The streetlights shine down through the darkening sky, sending circles of illumination onto the sidewalks and parking lot. I lead her to the passenger door of my Sonata.

"I expected you to drive a truck," she says.

"I used to. This is a hybrid and better on fuel economy." I open the door. "And isn't filled with mud."

Marilyn smiles as she sits down into the bucket seat.

I can't help but notice the shapeliness of her leg as her dress rides up. "I still can't believe you're here."

By the time I get around to the driver's seat, Marilyn is buckled in. "About this ex? Were you two serious?"

"Not really. Remember when I told you I'd taken a date to the dinner before I was hired?"

Nodding, I start the car. "Real but didn't last, is what you said."

She inhales and leans her head back against the seat. "His name is Bryce, Bryce Perkins. He also works at Parker and Stevens. We met during my internship. He works in talent acquisitions."

The car warms as we move into traffic. "So, he's involved in hires?"

"He's part of the team. I didn't think about it when you first asked me. I didn't think about it until earlier this afternoon when he asked me to accompany him to this same dinner."

My smile grows. "You decided to go through with this dinner to get back at him. You still like him."

"I don't still like him," she corrects. "He's boring

and narcissistic." Her smile blossoms. "I guess Devan had a point."

"What point would that be?"

"If I don't like someone, I forget about them."

"You didn't forget about me."

"That would be hard, seeing as we've been dating off and on."

Chapter Fourteen

Marilyn

"Besides," I say, "I agreed to go to this dinner before you were an ass. Your being an ass shouldn't have been a surprise. I stick to my word."

I'm also not sad about having Ricky at my side in front of Bryce. I truly give two shits about him, but the whole "no threat" comment hit me wrong. I'm not a threat, because I'm off and on again with someone a thousand times more interesting and exponentially more handsome.

"I owe you."

"You do."

For a moment, I take in Ricky's profile, protruding brow, high cheekbones, and strong, defined jaw. The years of working out in the elements have carved their way into his features, creating a rugged and handsome exterior. The physical labor has sculpted and toned his body in a way gyms are incapable of doing. In the masculine world, there are those who fit without trying and those who will never fit, no matter how much they try. Ricky Dunn fits.

Ricky pulls his car up to the front of the hotel. Reaching over to my arm, he grins. "I'll valet park. No sense making you walk across a parking lot in those shoes."

"If you think by being nice, I'll forget you're an ass, you're wrong."

He chuckles. "What can I say? I'm a nice ass."

A doorman opens my door and helps me to the sidewalk as Ricky gets out of the car to speak with the valet. Watching as he stands, I agree he has a nice ass.

Despite the cold winter chill and the way my breath forms small little clouds, the front of the Carmichael is stunning, bright, and inviting.

I stiffen for only a second, as Ricky lays his hand in the small of my back.

Dating.

Touching.

Letting out a breath, I tell myself again that I can do this.

Together, we walk into the lobby. The black-and-white tile floor shines, reflecting the large chandelier lights above. A sign points us up a grand staircase to the Parker and Stevens reception.

"Do you have any last-minute advice?" he asks as we begin our ascent.

"You want my advice? What was it you said…we've known each other since I was a kid."

Ricky lifts his hands. "Guilty as charged. Would it be weird to admit that I don't see the age difference the way I used to? And on top of that, when it comes to wealth management, you got your shit together long before me."

It isn't weird.

The age difference isn't as pronounced as it once was. I suppose that's silly, because the ten years haven't changed. Instead, we've changed. "Besides Herold Parker and Ralph Stevens, there will be multiple people from the talent acquisition team, most with dates or spouses."

"I'm glad I'm not walking in there alone."

"My advice is talk to as many people as possible. When they leave tonight, you want them to remember Richard Dunn."

After checking our coats, we enter the cocktail room. I peer around, seeing both familiar and unfamiliar faces. "See the older man over there, with the woman in the blue?" Ricky looks in the same direction. "That's Mr. Stevens."

As if he can hear me, which I'm relatively certain he can't, Mr. Stevens looks in our direction. His lips curl and cheeks rise.

"I'll introduce you," I volunteer as we approach the Stevenses.

"Ms. James," Mr. Stevens says with a nod. "What a nice surprise, seeing you here tonight. I'm confident we've already hired you."

"You have." I return his smile.

"Hello, Marilyn," Mrs. Stevens says.

"Hello. It's good to see you." I turn back to Mr. Stevens. "I'm such a satisfied employee, I've recommended Parker and Stevens to my"—I barely hesitate—"friend. Mr. and Mrs. Stevens, this is Richard Dunn."

Ricky and Mr. Stevens shake hands.

"Thank you for inviting me tonight," Ricky says.

I take a step back, observing as Ricky and Mr. Stevens carry on a conversation. A bit of pride comes to life inside me while listening to Ricky's responses. He's done his homework.

Mrs. Stevens steps closer and lowers her voice. "How do you know Mr. Dunn?"

Tearing my eyes away from the two men, I turn to

her and smile. “We come from the same hometown. We’ve known each other for most of my life.”

“He’s older than most of the applicants.”

“I’d say that’s a positive,” I respond. “He’s more likely to be a stable employee.”

“Oh, heavens. I didn’t mean it as a negative. Ralph mentioned his name.”

“I hope that’s good for Rich.”

“I would say by looking at the way the two are talking, it is good.”

A waiter stops with a tray of champagne flutes. I take two, a second for Ricky. Mrs. Stevens and I chat about something rather mundane. It isn’t until Ricky looks around that I excuse myself and step to his side.

“This is for you,” I say, offering him the glass.

“Thank you.” He turns back to Mr. Stevens. “I look forward to speaking about this in greater detail on Monday.”

“My assistant will set up a time.”

It isn’t until we step away that I ask excitedly, “What was that about? He wants to talk to you Monday?”

Ricky reaches for my hand. While the warmth of his touch travels through my bloodstream, I’m not sure he even realizes what he’s doing. “He asked me about my parents’ farm and what I did on it.”

“He asked you about the farm?”

"It seems that those individuals still fortunate enough to farm succeed due to their size and worth. Mr. Stevens wants to structure a financial wealth plan that would work for farmers. The income isn't as reliable as other professions, and there are a long list of variables. He wants someone who understands the business to work on the research and development."

"Oh my God, Ricky, that's fantastic. Research and development isn't outlined in the new starting position. This could be big."

Letting go of my hand, he wraps his arm around me and gives me a hug. "I owe this to you."

"No, you owe it to your hard work."

"Marilyn."

Ricky and I take a step apart and turn to the deep voice. I clench my teeth together at the sight of my ex-boyfriend. I force a smile. "Bryce, I see you made it."

It doesn't take two seconds before Ricky steps closer, no doubt remembering that this is my ex.

A woman appears at Bryce's side.

"Beth decided she was up to attending."

This is the woman who said I wasn't a threat.

I plaster a smile on my lips and offer her my free hand. "Hello, Beth. I'm Marilyn."

"Nice to finally meet you." Her focus isn't on me, but on Ricky.

I reach for his arm and lean closer. "Bryce and Beth, this is my date, Richard Dunn."

Everyone greets one another.

"Richard..." Bryce says. "Yes, I remember looking at your portfolio. I had no idea you knew Marilyn."

Ricky smiles down at me and back to Bryce. "For most of our lives—hers, at least."

When we step away, Ricky lowers his voice. "Obviously, you broke up with him. Because no one would pick her over you."

I scoff. "I think there've been four or five between me and Beth."

"He still likes you."

Remembering what Devan said about men I don't like, I grin. "Who was that again?"

By the time the dinner is complete and people are beginning to disperse, Ricky and I have made our way around the room, talking to the partners, members of the talent acquisition team, and other candidates. I hadn't considered Ricky's age until we met more of the candidates. Mrs. Stevens had a point about how young they all are.

Back at the coat check, Ricky helps me with my coat, leaning down and whispering in my ear. "I said I owe you. When would you like to collect?"

Warmth fills my cheeks, because I'm certain he's not thinking about the same kinds of reparations as I am. "No need. Take me home and we can wave to each other once you're working in the firm."

Ricky reaches for the lapels of my wool coat, tugging me closer, filling my field of vision until he's all I can see. "I don't want to wave at you."

Perhaps it's the alcohol we've consumed or the high from everyone's reaction to Ricky, but I've forgotten about last night, and my confidence is returning. "What do you want?"

"How about I take you out for a celebration?"

"Tonight?"

"Yeah, we could go to any of the restaurants around here."

"You could come to my place."

Ricky brings his lips together. "Are you inviting me?"

I nod. "No strings. Just a more private celebration."

Chapter Fifteen

Ricky

My heartbeat echoes in my ears, giving an erratic cadence to the otherwise silence within my car. Neither one of us has said much since we began driving. Peering to my right, I notice the way Marilyn's hands rest in her lap, the way she stares out the side window, and the way the sweet scent of her perfume fills my senses.

Standing at the coat check, I wanted to lean in and kiss her.

From the low I felt as I was dressing for the dinner to now, my emotions have taken a drastic swing, a pendulum of sorts. Part of me worries that another violent shift is in the making.

Private celebration.

If only I knew for sure what she was thinking.

It's kind of ridiculous that a thirty-five-year-old man is unsure where the night will go. With anyone else, I would catch whatever is being thrown my way. The thing is, Marilyn isn't anyone else. I don't want to fuck this up.

Parking outside her apartment building, I hurry around to the other side of the car. She has the door open; I swing it wider and offer her my hand. My fingers encase hers as she stands. The sounds of the chilled night disappear as she leans against me, her chin raised and soft lips pursed.

"I don't want to fu—"

Splaying her fingers against my chest, Marilyn pushes upward, silencing me with the sweet warmth of her kiss. I frame her cheeks with my hands, turning her face and deepening our kiss. All night long, I've dreamed of kissing her like this. It's been a hunger eating away at me, with each smile or comment she's given me. One or two steps, and I have her backed against my car, my hips pressing into hers.

Marilyn moves her hands upward, her fingers weaving through my hair.

She's as hungry for this as I am.

Unlike many years ago, there's no awkwardness, no fumbling with noses hitting or uncertainty.

She pulls back, catching her breath. "Come in?"

"I want that more than anything."

Marilyn reaches for my hand and leads me toward the apartment building. Once we're at her door, I wait while she unlocks the dead bolt. As soon as we're inside, I pin her against the door, one of my hands on the wooden barrier and the other around her waist, pulling her toward me.

We're fire and ice, two consenting adults lost in our private celebration. She tastes of sweetness and desire, our kisses lingering as we both try to rid ourselves of our winter covering. Our coats litter the floor as I start to lead her away.

I stop, looking around the dark living room. "I don't know where your bedroom is," I confess.

With a sparkle in her blue orbs, Marilyn takes my hand and leads me across the large room, opens a door wider, and steps into her bedroom. The room is in shambles, drawers open, shoes on the floor, and the bed is strewn with dresses.

"I couldn't decide what to wear."

I run my palm down her arm, scanning the dress she's wearing. "You were stunning tonight. But it wasn't the dress. It's you."

"You don't have to say things you don't mean."

I reach for her shoulders. "I mean every word. I know I've fucked up. I don't want to do it again."

Marilyn lays a finger on my lips. "We've talked enough, don't you think?"

"I want to be inside you."

She nods.

"What about tomorrow?" I ask.

"I don't know. I've been watching you all night. You have a future at Parker and Stevens. The partners think we're a couple." She tilts her head. "Maybe we should pretend a little longer—you know, in case they question."

I don't want to pretend.

I want to see where this could go.

"Is that what you want, to pretend?"

"Right now," she says, "I want what you said. I want you inside me. Just in case you're curious, I'm not a virgin."

My lips curl. "Show me."

Her eyes open wide. "Show you?"

I nod.

Spinning her around, I unzip the zipper that has been mocking me all night. Her dress parts, revealing her bra and panties. Marilyn turns, reaches for the neckline, and pushes the dress over her shoulders. It falls, creating a black pool around her shoes.

My focus is on the way her large round globes are confined in the lace cups. "It's a shame to keep them all locked up in there."

Her smile returns. "Maybe you can help them out."

I reach behind her, releasing the three fasteners. Her bra falls, and her breasts break free.

Our eyes meet before I lower my head, sucking one nipple and then the other. Her gasp fills the air. I don't slow until both nipples are rigid and standing to attention. Marilyn's head lolls back as I continue showing her breasts the attention they deserve.

She stands straighter and pushes my suit coat from my shoulders. The tie is the next to go. It's as she unbuttons my shirt that her fingers brush over my skin. Like the striking of a match, sparks tingle my flesh as she trails down my chest and abdomen, feeling each indentation along the way.

"Do you have a condom?" she asks as she unbuckles my belt.

"I have one."

Her smile is breathtaking. "Then we better make it count."

She drops to her knees, her attention on the button and zipper of my pants. As they fall to my ankles, I reach for her chin and encourage her to stand. The way she licks her lips makes me weak in the knees. "When I said I want to be inside you, I didn't mean your luscious mouth."

She sweeps the dresses from the bed onto the floor.

Kicking off my loafers, I step away from my pants. My boxer briefs are doing very little to keep my erection contained. Cupping Marilyn's firm ass in my grasp, I lift her until her legs are around my waist and her boobs are smashed against my bare chest. She's as light as a feather as I carry her toward the bed.

Our first time wasn't great for her. I've been recalling that night in more detail over the last few days. With her in my arms, I want to show her that it can be better. I want her screaming my name.

Laying her on the soft covers, I reach for her panties and pull them down. "These are sexy as hell," I say, referring to her high heels. "I think it's time to free your feet too."

As I unbuckle the tiny straps, Marilyn pulls some large pins from her hair, loosening her locks and allowing the dark waves to veil over her slender shoulders.

"You're more beautiful than I remember."

She reaches for my shoulder. "You're still as buff as I remember. I was afraid the world of numbers would make you soft."

"No, baby. I'm hard as a rock."

I suck in a breath as she lowers one hand and grasps my erection through my boxers.

"What are you going to do about that?" she asks.

"Nothing right now."

Her eyes widen. "Nothing?"

Tugging on her ankles, I cause her to lie back while pushing her knees upward. "First, I'm going to be sure you're ready."

"I'm ready." She sits forward and tries to push me back. "I've never come more than once in a night. I don't want to waste it on oral."

"Waste it? Someone's been doing it wrong." I arch my eyebrow. "Challenge accepted."

"Ricky."

"Trust me."

Slowly she nods, lies back on the pillow, and flops her arm over her eyes.

My hunger returns with a vengeance as I near her warm pussy and inhale her sweet scent. Holding her knees apart, I dive in, my tongue delving deep where my cock aches to be. Damn, she's already soaked. I lap her juices as she bucks beneath my hold. With two fingers in her tight chamber, I tantalize her swollen clit. I work her to a tizzy and back off. Listening to her noises, I could go on forever.

It isn't until her legs stiffen that I receive my reward. Her essence covers my lips and chin as she lets out a loud whimper. Slowly, I move up her body, taking my time and kissing the insides of her thighs, over her mound, her flat stomach, and up to the boobs

I want to investigate. When my nose meets hers, I bring our lips together.

She stares into my eyes. "I think I'm done."

"You're not."

Crawling off the bed, I find my pants and retrieve my wallet. There's one condom. I'm not sure how long it's been there. Hopefully, they don't expire. In less than a minute, I'm back between her legs, my hard cock ready to enjoy what my tongue already has.

Chapter Sixteen

Marilyn

I tell myself not to overthink. It's the worst thing I can do. Pushing the doubts and concerns of tomorrow out of my head, I demand of myself to live in the here and now. This present is what I've dreamed of.

Ricky's toned body is the flame, drawing me closer. I'm a moth hopelessly attracted to his presence and purposely not heeding the dangers. Beneath the tips of my fingers, I sense each and every indentation, each muscle and tendon in his wide shoulders as he presses his erection against my core.

He lifts his face and torso, his brown eyes swirling with desire as his stare intensifies. "Will you give me another chance?"

I blink, trying to understand his question. "Another...?"

"I fucking want you, more than I thought possible."

"I'm here." The ache between my legs is growing with need.

"Tell me to stop right now."

"Why would I do that?"

"Because if we go through with this, I'm not going to ghost you. You'll be stuck with me until you tell me to go."

An ache forms in my chest. "Don't make promises you don't intend to keep. I want this. Tomorrow is tomorrow. I want to live in today." My pleas must have been heard. All at once, I close my eyes and arch my back as Ricky's lips capture mine, and he plunges deep inside me. My body stretches to accommodate his presence.

Ricky's movements still. "Look at me, Marilyn."

I open my eyes, lost in a swirl of chocolate, dark and light.

"Are you okay?" he asks.

Swallowing, I nod. "You're bigger than I remember." I see his smile and the small dimples indenting his cheeks.

"You're as tight as I remember. Are you good?"

"I'm good," I say. "I have the feeling I could be

better if you stopped talking and did something with the massive cock currently in my pussy."

Ricky's laugh fills the room. "Oh, you want me to do something with my cock."

I lift an eyebrow. "If you're up to it."

To my utter shock and surprise, Ricky pulls out. Before I can verbalize my disappointment, he lifts my ass, encouraging me to turn. With my face on the pillow and ass in the air, Ricky slaps one cheek of my behind and then the other. The sting refocuses me. Without hesitation, he thrusts deeper than before, sending fireworks through my nervous system.

There's nothing gentle in what he's doing. The intense grip on my hips and the ferocity of his thrusts dominate my thoughts. Within me, anticipation begins to build, like adding heat to a pressure cooker. The friction is intense. For a moment, I think about what he's doing to my body. Tomorrow, I'll remember this with each step. Now, I don't want it to stop. The room fills with the sounds of two bodies, slapping and pounding. My entire body is on full alert.

Despite never having experienced anything like this, I'm captivated by the sensation of immense fullness. Ricky's curses fill my ears as synapse after synapse fires, the rattling of firecrackers before the explosive finale.

"Touch yourself," he says between kisses to my back and shoulders.

I do as he says, finding my clit while purposely touching the slickness of his cock.

"Fuck, Marilyn."

"Oh my God," I pant. My muscles constrict. Every muscle. From my scalp to my toes. The eruption is second only to Mount Vesuvius. My entire body trembles. The screams filling the room are familiar, yet foreign. It takes me a minute to realize that I'm the one screaming.

Ricky's deep roar comes moments later as his cock convulses within me.

With my body continuing to tremble, I collapse onto my stomach, unsure if I'm even capable of rolling. Ricky's weight covers me, our bodies still connected.

He tenderly eases my long hair away from my neck and gently peppers my cheek, my neck, and my shoulder with kisses. His voice breaks through the puddle that remains of my mind and body. "I think it's fair to say you came twice."

Opening my eyes, I meet his sparkling gaze. "I mean, it was okay."

Ricky slowly separates our union, leaving me with a sense of emptiness.

I feel the mattress move and hear him in the

attached bathroom, yet my body is still immobile. Thoughts of him leaving now threaten my orgasmic bliss, until he returns, a warm washcloth in hand.

"Roll over."

Shaking my head, I stifle a laugh. "I don't think I can move."

He helps me roll, until I'm on my back.

"I can take that," I offer.

Ricky shakes his head. "I'm responsible for that tight pussy being sore. I can take care of it."

Warmth fills my cheeks.

"Don't get all shy on me, Marilyn. Seconds before my cock was deep inside you, you were talking to make a sailor blush. I believe you said something about me doing something with my massive cock. I hope you weren't disappointed."

The entire time he's talking, he's tending to my mound, washing away my essence.

"You've improved," I say with a grin.

"It's really not fair to judge someone during your first time."

That fact brings back my unsettled feelings about our first time. "I knew you knew," I say, sitting up against the headboard.

Ricky tosses the washcloth onto the carpet and sits at my side. We're both completely nude as he pulls the sheet to our waists. I lift it to cover my breasts.

"You didn't tell me," he says, reaching for my hand and intertwining our fingers. "And when I realized, I freaked out."

A nod is my only response.

"I'm sorry. It was an important thing for you, and I treated it..." He exhales. "I'm not sure what I did. I ran scared." He lifts my hand and brings my knuckles to his lips. "I'm here now, if that counts for anything."

"You don't have to apologize any more. It's easier to hate you than to have you be nice."

"I don't want you to hate me."

"It's okay," I say, raising my shields. "Tonight was our celebration. No more and no less." I take a deep breath. "You can go if you want."

The shine in his brown eyes dims. "You don't trust me, and honestly, you have every reason not to. I'd like to stay. I have somewhere to be in the morning, but if you'll have me, I'll stay the night."

"I can get you blankets for the couch."

He lifts my hand and begins kissing, up to my elbow, to my shoulder, to the sensitive skin of my neck. With each flutter of kisses, goose bumps scatter in their wake. "I'd like to stay in your bed."

"I heard you snore."

Ricky grins. "That's hearsay, but you can let me know in the morning."

The childish dreams of my inner teenager spark to

life as Ricky wraps his strong arm around me, pulling me close and cradling my head on his hard shoulder. I tell myself it's not real. Ricky Dunn is just making up for what he did before.

Yet as his breathing evens and I find myself running my fingers over his wide chest and six-pack, the dreams of the teenager I once was seem real. It is almost as if I can touch him, sense my sore and satisfied core, and inhale his masculine scent.

I wake in a fog, the stiffness in my muscles reminding me of what Ricky and I did last night. A smile curls my lips at the memories of him at the dinner and the research and development Mr. Stevens discussed. I turn to my side, only to find the bed empty. A brush of the sheets tells me it's also cold.

Familiar uncertainty bubbles to life in my chest, reminding me that dreams don't come true. Not in real life. It isn't until I'm in the bathroom that I hear noises coming from the other end of my apartment.

Wearing panties and my short robe, I cautiously make my way toward the kitchen. The aroma of coffee beckons me.

I stop in the doorway, taking in the specimen of a man tending to something that smells like bacon on my stove. He's wearing low-riding blue jeans and no shirt as the meat in the frying pan spits and splatters. His hair is mused with a sexy bed head look, and his cheeks have more than their normal trimmed beard growth.

Crossing my arms over my breasts, I smirk.

Ricky turns, seeing me. "You are so fucking hot in that robe."

His compliment warms me from my head to my toes.

"I'm not used to half-naked men cooking me breakfast."

"Oh," he says, lifting the spatula. "Do you want breakfast too?"

"You weren't planning on feeding me?"

"I mean, if there's any left. You see, I worked up an appetite last night."

Shaking my head, I make my way barefoot to the coffeepot. As I'm pouring a cup, Ricky's warmth presses against my back as he wraps his hands around my waist, teasing the tie of my robe. "What do you think you're doing?"

His scruffy cheek comes to my neck, and his warm breath tickles my ear. "I'm worried that your tits are bound up again. I'm making it my life's work to assure their freedom."

Leaving the coffeepot and mug on the counter, I spin in his arms. "When I woke, I thought you were gone."

"You may not remember, with all the magnificent

orgasms you were having. I hear that can cause some temporary memory loss, but I told you if you didn't stop me, I was hanging around. You didn't." He steps back and grins. "Here I am."

We both turn to the smoke coming from the frying pan.

"Oh."

Ricky rushes to the pan, lifting it from the burner. "I hope you like your bacon crispy."

As I go to the refrigerator for my cream, Ricky again meets me. Before I can protest, he lifts me to the edge of the counter and reaches for the sash of my robe.

"What about breakfast?" I ask.

"The bacon needs to cool," he says with a lopsided grin as he tugs the sash, opening the material and exposing my breasts and panties. "After I saw you in this robe the other night, you have starred in every one of my wet dreams."

"You have wet dreams?"

"More like jack-off sessions in the shower, but the same idea."

He lowers his face to my breasts. The scratchiness of his beard growth sends zaps of electricity from my breasts to my core. I lean back on my outstretched arms, savoring the vision of him, his closed eyes and strong lips. My head falls backward. "Ricky."

He rains kisses lower, to the waistband of my panties.

"Ricky." My protest lacks sincerity.

"Fuck, Marilyn. You make me so damn hard."

I lift my behind as he pulls my panties lower, until they're on the floor. Ricky spreads my legs. "Your pussy is glistening." His chocolate-swirl stare comes my way. "One more time?"

"Condom?"

Ricky shakes his head. "No sex. Just let me taste you."

I slide from the counter and turn my back on him, purposely pressing my ass against his pinned erection. "I'm on the pill."

The sound of his zipper mixes with his thanks to a higher being, before his hand comes to the small of my back, pressing me forward as he moves my feet farther apart with his. I call out, biting my lip as he slides inside.

I've never agreed to unprotected sex. The pill is a backup.

My fingers search the smooth countertop for something, anything to grip. The sensation is too much. I can feel the way his cock hardens and moves. It's magical and all too addictive. I brace myself along the edge of the counter as Ricky thrusts and retreats, thrusts and retreats.

"Shit, Marilyn. I'm not going to last long."

"Me either." My body is already wound tight as a top. "This feels—" I push up on my tiptoes as Ricky slams into me, gripping my hips and panting against my neck. "So fucking good."

As he pulls out, our combined juices coat my thighs.

Ricky turns me around and lifts my chin. "Good morning, beautiful."

My focus is on his brown orbs; like the calming of a storm, the swirling has subsided. He has small lines next to his eyes, and his smile is bright. "Good morning."

His lips take mine. Strong and reassuring, his kiss is possessive and tender. "I'm usually more self-controlled."

"I'm not complaining." I peer over his shoulder. "What did you cook?"

"There are scrambled eggs in the microwave and toast. I wasn't sure how you liked your eggs."

A smile comes to my lips. "One of those things a boyfriend should probably know."

He tilts his head.

"Over medium," I say. "Runny yolk, but not the white."

"I'm over easy."

As we sit together at the breakfast bar and eat our

breakfast, Ricky asks me about my plans for the weekend.

"I told Devan I'd head down to Riverbend. Jill will be there for Todd's niece's birthday. She wants to have a tell-all." I give Ricky the side-eye. "It seems Devan found out I wasn't completely honest with her seven years ago."

"Shit. That's on me."

Of course, I knew that.

Chapter Seventeen

Ricky

"Is their knowing one of those instances I'm supposed to apologize for or not? I'm trying to keep up."

"Not," Marilyn says. "In a way, I'm glad the secret is out."

"What about last night?"

"And this morning," she says with a sexy grin.

I reach back and tug the hair tie from her long brown locks, watching as it cascades down her back and over her shoulders. "We could go for twice this morning."

She gathers her hair and twists it before flipping it over her shoulder. "I promised Devan I'd take off in the morning."

"Funny story."

Marilyn's blue eyes open wide. "What's funny?"

"Remember the backpack Kyla handed me last night? I was planning a trip to Riverbend. Justin asked me to come down to talk about his plans for the farms...I guess it's only one farm now—his."

"And Devan's."

I nod.

It's just weird after my whole life of my family owning our land that it is now part of the Sheers's farm. Knowing that my sister is still there makes it easier to take. An idea comes to life. "Do you want to ride down together?"

Marilyn coughs, choking on her coffee. "Together? Don't you think everyone will notice?"

"Yeah, but when we share a room at Devan's house, they'll probably notice that too."

Her head is shaking. "Whoa. I think you're moving a little fast."

Turning her barstool, I angle Marilyn until she's facing me. Stepping down to the floor, I spread her knees and move closer. "Let's scream it from the rooftops. Riverbend didn't implode when Justin and Devan announced their relationship. I think it can survive ours too."

"Ours."

Her cheeks have paled.

"Is this—" I motion between us "—not a relationship? I mean, if we were still in Riverbend, would you not want me to walk the stands before a softball game and kiss you?"

"Can we please go slower?"

"Slower, as in no more sex?"

She lays her hand on my chest. "Slower, as in telling our friends and family."

"Are you ashamed?" I ask.

"No," she answers quickly. "I'm confused."

I take a step back. "What are you confused about?"

"You."

"Can you be more specific?"

Marilyn hops down from the stool and paces to the sink and back with her lips pressed together. "What are you doing, Ricky Dunn?"

"I'm watching the most beautiful woman I know prance around in a sexy robe. I also just ate breakfast. It's not confusing."

"It is. Last night...this morning...I have no regrets."

"Fuck, that's encouraging."

She reaches for my arm. "Ricky, please. I'm not throwing it in your face, but you hurt me. I'm not even talking about your phone."

"I've changed that."

"You've heard the saying, hurt me once, shame on you. Hurt me twice, shame on me?"

Swallowing, I nod. "I don't want to hurt you."

"Did you want to seven years ago?"

"Intentionally, no."

"I don't want to hurt you either. Let's see where this goes. We can drive separately to Riverbend and sleep in separate rooms. Think of it as the opposite of last night. Instead of pretending we're a couple, let's pretend we're not. Just while we're in Riverbend."

"I don't like it."

Marilyn tilts her head and pouts her adorable lips, melting my resolve.

"Okay, but if I find you alone, I get to kiss you."

"If you find me alone, you can do more than that."

"Deal."

By early afternoon, I'm looking around the old barn, seeing that not much has changed. Devan and Justin have done so much with the house, the barn is probably not high on their priority list. Justin walks to the back tool bench and slides a wooden partition to the side, revealing a small refrigerator. He opens the door, takes out two beers, and slams the door shut. "Here." He tosses the beer my direction.

I'm lucky enough to catch it. "It's barely noon."

Justin hikes himself up on top of the workbench and opens his can. The shoosh fills the air. "It's five o'clock somewhere." Instead of taking a drink, he sets the can at his side and crosses his arms over his chest.

"You slept with one of Devan's best friends and then made her mad again. I feel alcohol is appropriate."

Shrugging, I open my can. "It's light beer. Almost like drinking water." I take a drink.

"I'm waiting."

I look at my friend. "I told you what happened on the phone. Devan's graduation party. Everything was consensual, but after I realized she'd never..." Saying the words brings back my feelings of self-loathing.

"You ran like a little girl."

Pressing my lips together, I give that a thought. "No, the little girl didn't run. She faced me every time with a smart remark or a sassy smirk. I ran like a coward. I didn't see that then, but I do now."

Justin picks up his beer and takes a slug. "Better late than never. I can't believe she came through for you on the partner dinner."

I feel the way my cheeks rise, but I can't seem to stop them. "Not as shocked as I was when I opened my apartment door. It was like a fucking angel descended from heaven to save my sorry ass. And she did too. She introduced me to everyone. I even have a telephone meeting with one of the partners on Monday. He wants to pick my brain about managing agricultural wealth."

"There's wealth in agriculture?"

"When you don't spend all your available cash on home renovations."

Justin shrugs. "It makes Devan happy. It makes me happy to live in a real home, not one of those McMansions."

"It looks great. You two worked your asses off."

"Speaking of ass, are you going to tell me when you last got some?"

My eyes bug out as I cough. "Fuck, no. And don't go sharing your sex life. Devan's still my sister, and I haven't completely ruled out that punch I offered years ago."

"Statute of limitations. I should kick your ass for Marcus."

That makes me laugh. "Marcus James. I don't think you will go out of your way for him."

Marcus is three years younger than us and a real conceited ass. On the football team, he thought he was the GOAT. One day after practice, Justin and I may have been involved in a prank to make him eat grass. The memory makes me smile as I take another drink of my beer.

"It was Devan's idea for us to invite you both here," Justin says, "assuming you didn't kill each other last night."

"Nope," I say, knowing that if I would have died last night, it would have been from my increased blood pressure while fucking a beautiful, sassy brunette.

"Do you think Marilyn will turn around and go home when she realizes you're here?"

"I hope not."

Justin's brow furrows. "You hope not?"

My smile breaks free. "I was an ass before, but now, ten years difference in age doesn't matter. Hell, she's accomplished more than I have. I'm amazed by her knowledge and am growing fond of her smart mouth. Of course" *—this is the part Marilyn and I discussed—* "she would rather never see me again. Maybe this is fate."

"Do you think the two of you could...?"

"The world beyond Riverbend is lonely. I said it. I'm a pansy."

Justin jumps down from the workbench. "You're not. Riverbend was lonely before Devan. I can't imagine being out with total strangers. At least here is here."

"I don't mind the strangers. I'd just also wouldn't mind a friendly—beautiful smile."

"Fuck." He comes closer and downs the rest of his beer. "You've got it bad."

"That's what Kyla said."

"Who the hell is Kyla?"

"My roommate's sister. She was at our apartment

yesterday. I was floundering, so I asked her for advice." Something occurs to me. "I seem to remember when there was this asshole who kissed a girl at a hog roast and went on about her for weeks. Didn't he have it bad?"

"He did, but he also was at a disadvantage. He didn't know the name of the BK—best kiss. You know Marilyn's name."

"I don't want to fuck this up."

Justin nods. "That's good. Maybe you won't this time." He looks out the dusty window. "I see Marilyn's car. Let's head into the house."

"Or we could have another beer."

Justin reaches for my arm. "Man up."

"Wait? Are you hiding beer from my sister? Let's talk about who's a man."

"Not hiding it. She knows about it. Some evenings, we come out here, grab a beer, climb up into the hayloft—"

"Stop," I interrupt. "TMI."

Justin laughs as we walk toward the back door of the house.

Chapter Eighteen

Marilyn
An hour and a half earlier

I text Devan, telling her I'm on my way. Ricky left for Riverbend thirty minutes earlier, after one more round of sex. The last time was in the shower. While I hadn't expected him to join me, I didn't exactly protest. The lack of condom usage adds a level of spontaneity that is exciting. Although it's hard to tell by the perpetual smile on my face, I have sore muscles in places I forgot existed.

I keep telling myself not to get my hopes up. By the reflection of the smiling fool in the rearview mirror, I'm not listening to my own advice. Instead of reliving each and every moment of the last twenty-four hours, I sync my phone and turn up a new album by a popular musician, singing along at the top of my lungs about a sign on his heart being reserved for me.

Barren trees pass by the windshield of my car as I drive along highways and narrow roads, making my way out of the world I've chosen back into the one where I was born and raised. Nothing much has changed in Riverbend since I visited for the holidays. Driving down Main Street, I pass Quintessential Treasures, the Main Street Diner, and see the names of familiar staples. Even on a cold Saturday in January, people are walking up and down the sidewalks.

It's another ten minutes before I make my way out to Devan and Justin's farm. The fields are plowed and frost-covered. I know from experience that winter wheat is waiting to make its sprouts visible. Turning down their lane, I pass the white barn, remembering all the fun times Devan, Jill, and I had in the dusty old structure.

As I pull up to their house, I notice Ricky's Sonata parked by Justin's old truck. After parking, I brace myself for a more difficult role than playing Ricky's date last night—pretending there's nothing between us, other than the partner dinner. Since we'd told everyone about the dinner, there is no use denying it happened.

Carrying my overnight bag, I head toward the house, taking in all the changes since Devan and Justin took ownership. The big front porch is still present with the pillars. A plume of smoke snakes through the sky from the chimney, filling the cool air with the aroma of burning wood. Instinctively, I reach for the doorknob, not bothering with knocking.

As a child, this home and Jill's were my second and third homes. We all entered one another's homes without knocking. Some things don't change.

"Devan," I call as I push the front door inward. I'm met with the warm, fire-heated air and a living room I barely recognize.

"Marilyn!" Devan screams, racing down the front staircase.

Dropping my overnight bag, I lift my arms and brace for impact. We hug as if it's been years and not months since we saw each other.

When Devan pulls back, her smile fades. "No more lying to your best friend." She looks even more forlorn. "Jill knew."

It isn't exactly an accusation, but I am done telling untruths—mostly. "He's your brother, Dev." I reach for her hand. "Can't you understand how bad I felt?"

"He didn't...take advantage...did he?"

I shake my head. "No. Nothing like that."

She scrunches her nose. "How was last night's dinner? I can't believe you decided to go with him."

Unbuttoning my coat, I feign a slight smile. "I

think it went well. Ricky really knows his stuff, and I think the partners were impressed. One even asked to talk to him about a position above the one he's interviewing for."

"Oh, he didn't say a word."

I look around at the new furniture and decorations. Even some of the layout is different. "I can't believe all the work you two have done."

Devan spins a complete circle. "Isn't it great?"

"It really is."

After I drop my coat on the sofa, Devan takes my hand. "Let me show you around."

Before moving, I ask, "Where is Ricky? I saw his car."

"Oh, that was supposed to be a surprise."

I lift my eyebrows.

"You're not leaving now?" she asks.

"I'm not. But don't try to play matchmaker." I cross my arms over my chest. "Help with the dinner and that was it. No strings."

Devan's gaze sparkles. "No one is talking strings. Just think how great it would be if you and Ricky worked things out. We could be sisters."

"If you say sister wives, I'm driving away and never coming back."

Devan laughs. "Jill said she'll be over after the birthday party." She motions for me to follow her, leading me upstairs. Opening the first door on the right at the top of the stairs, she says, "This is where you'll sleep." She points across the hallway. "That's our room. And Ricky is staying in this room. The last one is still my office."

As we pass by the room Devan labeled as Ricky's, I see his backpack on the bed. It's the same one he had at my apartment. To avoid more conversation about Ricky, I change the subject. "I'm a little surprised there's not a nursery."

Devan presses her lips together. "We're talking about kids."

"Has no one told you that's not how you get them?"

"We've both been around Jill forever. I think she started telling us the birds and bees in third grade."

"Oh, I hope it wasn't that young. Middle school."

We both laugh as the slam of the back door screen rattles the house.

"Some things never change," I say.

"We kept the door for sentimental reasons, and my mom was right, it's more effective than a security system."

"Devan," Justin's voice booms from the first floor. "We're back."

"We?" I ask.

"Justin and Ricky," Devan says with a grin.

Let the pretending begin.

I follow Devan as we take the back staircase, the one that leads to the kitchen. It's nearly impossible not to make eye contact with Ricky, especially with how sexy he looks in his faded blue jeans and green thermal, one that hugs his arms and shoulders, showing off his muscles. Instead, I focus on the kitchen itself.

"Oh my God, this kitchen is to die for."

What had once been a large room with country cabinets and Formica countertops is now modern. The wooden cabinets have been replaced by tall white ones above the counter and bright-blue ones below. The countertops are hard surface, and beneath the upper cabinets are LED lights, glowing a faint blue onto the white subway-tile backsplash. The appliances are all new, and now there's a large island, containing the stovetop and a breakfast bar. A glass four-season room has been added to the back of the house, expanding the room for a kitchen table.

I spin around, stopping as I look at my best friend. "This kitchen is unbelievable. Jill said you'd done a lot, but wow. This looks like it belongs in a magazine."

Devan hugs Justin's arm. "It seems that Justin is a great carpenter too."

"It's always good to have something to fall back on," I say with a smirk.

Justin laughs. "If someone else is covering the cost,

I could be talked into doing more. Right now, I'm pretty busy planning for spring." He turns to Ricky. "That's why Ricky is here."

"It's not for your carpentry skills?" I ask Ricky with all the sass I can muster.

"I can swing a hammer with the best of them," he responds.

"That will be helpful with Parker and Stevens."

Ricky flashes a thousand-watt grin. "My skills aren't limited."

"Hmm," I say, turning to Devan. "Did you stock up on cider?"

"And cinnamon."

My focus goes to Justin. "What are you two planning on doing while we have our girls' night?"

Justin looks at Ricky, who lifts his eyebrows. "Guess we're hanging out."

"No," Devan and I say together.

She lays her hand on Justin's arm. "It's hard to *talk* with others around."

"Are you telling all your secrets?" Ricky asks.

"Only the most salacious," Devan replies.

Justin taps Ricky's shoulder. "We can go to my office and look over my plans for spring. I'd like your opinion." He looks back at Devan. "And then we can head to Decoy Ducks. I'll call some of the other guys. They'll be happy to see Ricky."

"That makes someone," I mutter under my breath. I spot my overnight bag on the living room floor. "I'm going to take this upstairs. Then I'll be back down."

"It's early for cider, but I'll get us some lemonade," Devan says.

I take one last look at the three of them in Devan's kitchen before heading up the front staircase. With each step, I remind myself that Ricky walked away from me once and he could easily do it again.

There's just that small part of me that wishes.

"Wishes are for children," I mumble as I take the overnight bag into the bedroom Devan assigned. It was hers when she was younger, and despite the renovations, my mind is flooded with memories.

Stepping out of the room, I turn toward the kitchen staircase and run into a brick wall. Literally, run into... Ricky reaches out and grasps my arm, stopping me from falling on my ass. The vise grip of his hold reminds me how tight he held to my hips. Biting my lower lip, I look up, meeting his gaze.

Chapter Nineteen

Ricky

"What are you doing?" Marilyn asks.

"I don't like this. We're here to come clean to our friends, so why are we lying to them?"

"Are we?" Her beautiful blue eyes glisten.

Even the thought of Marilyn crying is too much. Releasing her arm, I pull her to me, smashing her breasts against my chest as I move us into the room with Marilyn's overnight bag on the floor and close the door. When she looks up, I see red splotches on her neck and cheeks.

"Talk to me."

Marilyn's nostrils flare. "I think it would be easier to admit that we're not right for each other."

"Easier?" I ask, my volume increasing. "What the fuck is easier about that?"

"I don't want to be hurt, Ricky." She pushes away from me and walks to the window. With her back turned, she continues talking. "During my drive down here, my thoughts were all stupid and unobtainable." She spins toward me. "I've liked you since I was a kid." She motions between us. "This isn't real."

Fuck that.

I take two long strides and meet her chest-to-chest, towering over her. "This is real, Marilyn." Snaking one arm around her waist, I bring the other to her long hair and tug it back, making her lift her perfect pouty lips to mine. Before she can say anything, my kiss captures her, stealing her protest.

I kiss her like there's no tomorrow, because if she keeps listening to the voices in her head, there won't be a tomorrow. I press my tongue against the seam of her lips, demanding entrance. Once inside her warm heaven, our tongues slide and twist, a tango of give-and-take. The longer we kiss, the slacker she becomes in my arms, the tension easing from her. My hand around her waist goes lower, over her firm ass, pulling her toward me.

When I come up for air, I meet her radiant blue orbs. "This is real."

"I want it to be."

"Then stop fighting it."

Her lips quiver as she leans her forehead against my chest.

Framing her cheeks, I lift her face back to mine. "Tell me when I've lied to you."

Marilyn's eyes close and open. "You haven't."

"I know I hurt you. There's no fucking excuse for that. There was no lying. We went into that night after graduation with a deal for no strings." I stare deep into her gaze. "I want strings, one or two, a whole fucking spool. I don't know what our future holds, but I know that I want to give it a try. And that means not lying to our friends. Not lying to each other." My cheeks rise. "I fucking love your sassy mouth, but I don't want those sassy remarks to sound like you hate me again."

Marilyn's voice is barely a whisper. "I'm not sure I ever hated you."

"What was that? I didn't hear you."

She sniffles before speaking louder. "I hated that you didn't think about me the way I thought of you."

"Do you want to know what I think of you right this minute?"

She shrugs. "I don't know. Do I?"

"I think you do." Releasing her, I reach for her hands, holding both of them in mine. I tug her toward the bed, sit, and pull her onto my lap.

"I'm too heavy."

Not allowing her to get up, I hold her close. "You're light as a feather." For a long moment, I'm silent, just looking at her—really looking. It's as if I'm seeing her in a new light after knowing her for so long.

Letting go of her hands, I brush a rogue strand of her long hair behind her ears. One side and then the other. My gaze begrudgingly leaves her stunning stare and lowers, inch by inch. Instead of seeing the soft blue sweater, I imagine what she looks like beneath, her perfect boobs free from their prison. Lower, I imagine the way her hips curve, the way her trim stomach tightens as she comes. I stop myself before making it to her warm, wet pussy.

If I don't, we'll have to come up with another explanation for Justin and Devan.

"Last night," I begin, "I asked you to give me another chance. You didn't answer."

"Because I don't understand what you're asking. We never dated before."

"We never dated because I was scared."

Marilyn cups my cheek. "Am I that scary?"

"Yes." I nod with a grin. "All those years ago, I was me, a twenty-eight-year-old with nothing to show for my life but dirt under my fingernails and work that never ended." When she tries to speak, I place a finger on her lips. "You, on the other hand, had been accepted to Ball State. You had a plan for your life. I wasn't looking for a relationship, but if I had been, I wouldn't have looked at you." I hurry to keep her from questioning. "Not because you aren't the most beautiful woman I know, but because I didn't deserve you—probably still don't. You had your whole life in front of you. You were never shy about wanting to get out of Riverbend."

Marilyn reaches for my hand and turns it over, inspecting my nails. "No dirt."

"Not now, but there will be. I'll do what I can to help Justin. He has twice the acreage now, and he's not only my friend but my brother-in-law."

"You deserve to be happy with whomever you see in your future."

"It's taken me too damn long, but I see you, Marilyn. I want to deserve you. Farming is an honorable profession. My dad and Justin's dad did it before us. I would never diss what Justin does, but I wasn't fulfilled. I don't know if I will be at Parker and Stevens, but I think I could be." I drop a kiss on her upturned nose. "We should address the obvious. I'm a decade older than you. Years ago, our ages bothered me, but they don't anymore. Do they bother you?"

She shakes her head. "I think I've gotten used to them. Last night, Mrs. Stevens mentioned you are older than the other applicants. I hadn't thought about that until she said it."

My forehead furrows. "Did she say that was bad?"

A smile threatens Marilyn's lips, curling the ends. "She agreed it made you more stable. And by the sound of what Mr. Stevens proposed to you, he sees your life experiences as assets that you can bring to Parker and Stevens."

Rubbing her back, I ask the same question I've been asking since last night, "Will you give me another chance?"

"You're scary too."

"I am?" I ask with a grin.

Marilyn nods. "I'm afraid to trust you."

"You trusted me with your body last night."

"And today."

"And today," I say, smiling.

"My body isn't as easily hurt as my heart."

I lay my hand over her sweater. "If you think I'd ever hurt what's protected by these amazing boobs, intentionally," I add, "you don't know me. I'd like to get to know you better and vice versa."

"That means telling our friends the truth?"

"I think it does."

"Okay."

Our lips come together, a kiss sealing our agreement and increasing my circulation. When she pulls slightly away, I tip my chin down. "Unless we want

Devan and Justin to wait longer, I suggest we head downstairs."

"Do you think they'd mind if we were another thirty minutes?"

Holding her securely, I spin, lowering her to the bed and leaning over her. Marilyn's giggles fill the air, and her smile radiates her change in emotion. When she looks up at me surrounded by a cloud of her soft hair, I am taken by how much I truly want this to work.

"I think we should go downstairs," she says.

Cupping her chin, I run my thumb over her puffy lips. "I prefer your smile."

"I prefer smiling."

I stand and reach for her hand. "Ready to come clean?"

"Are you proposing another shower, because I'm game."

Damn. This woman.

"Many future showers. Devan and Justin first."

"I'm as ready as I'll ever be."

Chapter Twenty

Marilyn

With my hand in Ricky's, we make it down the back stairs. The newly renovated kitchen is beautiful, but devoid of people. Together, we walk through the first floor, the dining room and the living room. At each turn, I expect to see our friends. We find nothing but silence. Finally, we make it to the front office. For most of my life, it belonged to Devan's dad, Jack. Now, I suppose it is Justin's.

The door is closed.

Ricky looks my way, silently shrugging. I nod. Instead of knocking, he opens the door and grumbles. "Jeez, get a room."

Peering around his shoulder, I smile, seeing Devan

sitting on Justin's lap, not unlike how Ricky and I were a few minutes ago.

Devan laughs, throwing her head back. "Since you two went MIA, we decided to give you space." Her attention goes to where my hand is in Ricky's. "It looks like you weren't upstairs fighting."

Despite the warmth filling my cheeks, I walk around Ricky and face our friends. "This weekend is about coming clean, right?"

"Shower is upstairs," Justin says, causing my cheeks to flame even brighter as memories of this morning's shower take new life in my mind.

Devan stands, separating herself from her husband. "Okay, spill. Both of you."

I look up at Ricky as he stares down at me. Taking a breath, I'm the first to speak. "Maybe I'm an idiot, but we are going to give this a try."

"This...?" Devan presses.

Ricky volunteers, "What Marilyn is saying is that she's giving me another chance, one I hope I don't blow."

"That question I asked earlier..." Justin says to Ricky.

"Still none of your business."

With a contented grin, Justin nods. He looks at me. "Just so you know, Marilyn, Rick never said anything to me about..."

"About our first time," I say.

Devan's eyes grow wide. "Does that mean there's been a second, a third…?"

Ignoring the fire raging in my cheeks and neck, I smile at my friend. "It means two consenting adults are going to see if we can make this work."

"That means you're dating?" Devan asks.

Again, Ricky and I look at each other and nod. Ricky lets go of my hand and wraps his arm around my shoulder. "If we need labels, then yes, at least until Marilyn realizes she's too good for me."

Devan's scream fills the office as she claps her hands. "I knew it. I knew you didn't really hate each other. I mean, I knew after Justin told me what happened. Before then, you had me fooled." She reaches for my hand. "Come on, let's go to the kitchen, and you can tell me everything."

Ricky tugs on my other hand, leans down, and kisses me. It isn't the same as getting a pregame kiss in the stands before a Riverbend men's softball game, but in many ways, it feels as significant. I smile up at him. "Dating?"

"Yeah. I like the sound of that."

"Me too."

It isn't until Devan has us back in the kitchen that she turns, grabs my arms, and jumps up and down, mouthing a silent scream. Finally, she speaks. "This is amazing."

"You don't think it's weird that your friend likes your brother?"

"Yes. But to be honest, I would think it was weird that anyone liked Ricky. I think it's fantastic that he likes you too. He's never seemed like the settle-down type."

Settle down.

That's not what we're doing.

Dating.

Yep, just dating.

Devan and I keep the conversation light until Justin and Ricky leave the house. They claimed they had a few things to check out in the barns, and then they were meeting some friends in town at Decoy Ducks, one of Riverbend's most popular drinking establishments.

Once the back door slams, she reaches across the table and covers my hand with hers. "Give me details." She scrunches her nose. "Not copious amounts, because Ricky is my brother, but still."

"You're no longer mad?"

"I guess it helped that Justin didn't know either. Sounds like my brother's not the type of ass who tells the whole world. Point for him, right?"

"We've talked about it, something we hadn't done…ever."

"I hope you made him grovel."

That makes me smile. "I didn't make him, but he's done a good job. I'm scared to believe him. That's why we agreed to pretend to not be involved." I sigh. "I don't want to have to face you or the rest of Riverbend if he hurts me again."

"You both knew the other was going to be here?"

"Yeah. I mentioned that I was headed down here, and he told me Justin asked him to come down."

"When?"

"This morning." My eyes grow wide as soon as the answer is past my lips.

"This morning," Devan says a bit too loudly. "Is that…because you two were together since last night?"

Covering my face with my hands, I lean forward.

"You were!" she shouts excitedly. "Does that mean there's been a second or third time?"

"Fourth," I confess through the protection of my hands.

We both startle and turn at the slamming of the screen door. Jill steps inside with two reusable grocery bags, overflowing with wine bottles and a plethora of snacks. "I'm here. What did I miss?" She sets the bags on the kitchen table and looks at me. "I brought wine and snacks in case we have a broken heart to mend."

Devan looks at me, and we both giggle.

"Oh shit," Jill says. "Not a broken heart?"

I shake my head. "Not yet."

"Okay, reason to celebrate. We can drink to being happy and childless. That birthday party was torture." She turns to Devan. "Your nieces were there."

"They're not torture."

"They are when they're part of a twenty-five-kid-strong gang of squealing, screaming children high on sugar and jacked up on party games."

I stand. "It sounds like Jill needs the wine." I look around the now, unfamiliar kitchen. "I don't even know where your wine openers are anymore."

Soon, we all have a glass of wine and are sitting in front of Devan's fireplace. It is the original fireplace, made by her grandpa or great-grandpa when the house was first constructed. Honestly, it's pretty cool that the Dunns have had this home in their family for so long. It makes me understand what Ricky was saying about being glad that his dad sold the farm to Justin and Devan.

It's still in the family.

Outside the windows, snowflakes dance in the air. There aren't enough to cover the ground, but enough to remind us that it's winter in southern Indiana. Inside their home, the fire is warm and comforting. Sitting on a love seat, I bend my legs beneath me and listen to Jill go on about the birthday party.

It's right as she starts to lament spending the night at the Blakelys' instead of with her parents that she looks at me. "Wait, why am I talking?"

Devan and I laugh.

"What's happening with you and Ricky?"

"Crazy, wild sex," Devan volunteers.

"I never said it was crazy or wild."

This time, it's Jill's screech that threatens to break our wineglasses. "I need a play-by-play on how you went from hating him to wild and crazy sex."

Twisting the stem of my glass between my fingers, I think about the last twenty-four hours. "I suppose I haven't hated him as much as I said. I hated what he did or didn't do."

"And you've forgiven him?" Jill asks.

"Yes and no."

"No?" Devan asks.

"I was hurt because he didn't do anything after our one time."

Devan wiggles four fingers.

Jill gasps.

"The first time," I clarify. "We both went into sex declaring it wasn't a big deal. No strings. I guess it was a big deal, but only to me. I thought he might think so too, but he didn't. He stuck to our agreement. That wasn't fair of me to be upset because he did what I said. In that way, he doesn't need my forgiveness."

"What's changed?" Jill asks.

"Besides seven years..." My friends listen as I try to make sense out of what doesn't make sense. Somehow after hearing Ricky's explanation, I see things differently. Never in a million years would I have thought he felt undeserving of me. With the changes he's made in his life over the past few years, his reasoning falls into place.

"Tell us about the partner dinner," Devan says.

"I wasn't going to go." My eyes open wide. "Oh, Jill, you don't know this part."

"Why am I always the last to know?"

Devan presses her lips together. "Excuse me. Seven years late in learning, here."

I jump in before my friends battle over who is told less. "Thursday night, Ricky and I went to dinner to prepare for our fake date on Friday. We had a good time." I smile at Jill. "He isn't boring."

"How many languages does he speak?" Jill asks.

"One, to my knowledge." I go on with my story. "At the end of the evening, I ask for his phone. He wanted my address. As I began to add my name, it came up—"

"With a note," Devan adds.

"Something like 'great in bed'?" Jill asks.

I shake my head. “Marilyn J. Do not answer.”

“Oh,” Jill growls. “And you still went to the dinner with him?”

“I wasn’t going to. I was mad. Except, later that night, he showed up at my apartment with a pint of caramel ice cream.”

Both of my friends swoon.

“I still didn’t forgive him. I ate the ice cream in the bathtub with wine.” They both sigh. “Then the next day at work, I receive a handwritten letter from him, asking for forgiveness and telling me to forget the dinner.” I take a drink of my wine. “I was going to, but then Bryce came into my office.”

Jill’s nose wrinkles. “Ugh. Why?”

“He’s on the talent acquisition team and had to go to the dinner, and his current girlfriend wasn’t feeling well.”

“He asked you to go with *him*?” Jill’s tone goes up an octave.

Pressing my lips together, I nod. “And get this, it was his girlfriend’s idea. She said he should take me, because I wasn’t a threat.”

Both of their mouths open wide.

“Bitch,” Jill mutters under her breath.

“I decided I wanted to be there, with a better plus-one than Bryce.”

“I never met him,” Devan says.

Jill responds, "You aren't missing much. Real douchebag."

"Did you tell Ricky about Bryce?"

"I told Ricky that Bryce asked me to the dinner, but there is nothing between us." A smile comes to my lips. "Seeing the two of them side by side makes me wonder what I ever saw in Bryce."

Devan shakes her head. "Still my brother."

"Now," Jill says, "tell me about numbers two, three, and four."

It's my turn to shake my head. "Nope. I'll just say that he's a lot better than before. A whole lot."

"And it doesn't hurt that you're more experienced," Jill says, lifting her glass.

"It's not like I have an extensive list, but of the few..." I let out a long sigh. "I could get used to Ricky."

"This is awesome," Devan says. "You could become my sister."

"I'm not making any predictions."

Devan stands and lifts her glass. "I am. I predict a summer wedding."

Jill stands in alliance. "To a summer wedding."

"Come on," they both say, encouraging me to stand.

I lift my glass. "To not getting my heart broken."

We all clink glasses.

Chapter Twenty-One

Marilyn

Sunday morning, Devan, Justin, Ricky, and I sit around Devan's kitchen table, talking and laughing in a way that seems too good to be true. It's casual and comfortable, the men in their nylon shorts and T-shirts, and Devan and me in our pajamas with our hair pulled back in ponytails. For the two of us, it's like when we lived together. Sunday mornings were always our together time.

Unlike in our apartment in Muncie, it's not only the two of us. Every now and then, Ricky reaches out, squeezing my knee or taking my hand. Together, Devan and I made a breakfast of eggs, bacon, and pancakes.

Justin adds another stack of pancakes to his plate.

"How many is that?" Ricky asks, leaning back with his coffee mug.

"I'm not counting, asshole," Justin replies with a smile. "I remember you out-eating me at every meal."

Ricky pushes his plate away from the edge of the table. "Those days are over. Sitting at a desk doesn't burn enough calories to eat like that."

Devan laughs. "We both like to cook, and it's good to know it will be eaten."

"You cook?" Ricky asks Justin.

"Yeah. I bet you do too, or you're starving in that apartment."

"I cook," Ricky admits, "but not well. Eating out all the time gets old and expensive." He turns to me. "Do you cook?"

"Is this a deal-breaker?" I ask with a grin, lifting my coffee mug to my lips. "You made me breakfast yesterday. I could get used to that."

"Deal. I cook breakfast and you cook dinner."

"Oh," Devan says with raised eyebrows. "Are we talking about cohabitation?"

"No," Ricky and I say in unison.

Again, he reaches for my knee. "Maybe spending the night now and then?"

"I can't wait to meet Max."

Justin rolls his eyes and stabs a giant bite of pancakes.

"What?" I ask. "His sister seems nice enough."

"I didn't even know he had a sister until Friday morning," Ricky replies. "Waking up to strange, as in unfamiliar and sometimes odd, women in my apartment is a recurring theme."

It's my turn to lift my eyebrows. "How often does Max meet your dates the next morning?"

"I can say, unequivocally, never." When I don't respond, he continues, "I've been busy with classes, homework, and my brain-numbing job at the mall."

"Hopefully, you'll be able to quit that job soon." I lift my hand, crossing my fingers.

Justin looks between me and Ricky. "Do you think it's a good idea to work together?"

We both shrug.

"Why not?" I ask.

"It's a lot of togetherness."

"Not really," I say. "I have my own office, and depending on what Ricky—excuse me, *Rich*—is hired to do, he could be in a completely different part of the building." I smile his way. "It might be nice to have lunch together now and then."

"Don't you and Jill meet for lunch sometimes?" Devan asks.

"We do. Her law firm isn't far from Parker and Stevens."

Devan sighs. "I miss you two. It was great being together last night."

"You can always come up to Carmel. We can do a girls' night at my place." I look around. "It isn't as big as your home, but the three of us will fit."

Devan stands to clear the table. I'm a second behind her.

"No," Ricky says. "You two made this delicious breakfast. Justin and I will clean the kitchen."

Devan laughs. "Justin cooks. He doesn't clean the kitchen."

Justin hurriedly chews the last of his pancakes. "We have this. Go, do whatever you need to do."

Devan and I look at each other. "Okay, then," she says. "I'll shower."

"Let me know when you're done," I say.

"Justin installed those instant hot water heaters in each of the bathrooms. We can shower at the same time and both have hot water."

"Fancy," I say with a smile. "All right, boys. Have fun."

Ricky reaches for my hand and tugs me closer. With his lips mere millimeters from mine, he whispers, "Don't lock the door."

Heat sets my cheeks ablaze as I shake my head.

His lips brush mine. Without his saying another

thing, his eyebrows jump, and the different shades of brown swirl in his eyes.

By the time I make it up the back staircase, leaving the bathroom door unlocked is all I can think about. I wondered if we would sleep together last night, but Ricky and Justin weren't back by the time Jill left, and I was exhausted. When I woke this morning, there was a note on the pillow next to mine.

I want to wake you, but you're too damn cute sound asleep. Instead, I'll dream of you.

(Heart)

Yours,

Ricky

I tucked the note into my overnight bag.

Taking my things into the bathroom, I close the door. My concentration is on the small button in the middle of the doorknob. Time passes as I put my shampoo and other supplies in the shower, turn on the water—which is quickly nice and hot—and strip out of my pajamas. This shower isn't like mine at my apartment. It's the kind that is also a bathtub with a shower curtain.

The more I look at it, the more I realize it won't be conducive to two.

Stepping into the tub, I let the hot water flatten and soak my hair. It's as I'm lathering the shampoo that I hear the bathroom door open. Peeking from behind the shower curtain, I look out, meeting Ricky's sexy grin.

"I don't think there's room in here," I say.

Biting my lip, I watch as he pulls his T-shirt over his head, revealing his toned abdomen and bulging biceps. The nylon shorts sit low on his hips, exposing a trail of brown hair that disappears under his shorts.

Without hesitation, Ricky tugs the shorts down.

My eyes grow wide at the glorious sight of him fully nude. I sweep my gaze from his muscular legs up to his semi-erect penis and higher still, settling on his sparkling chocolate orbs.

"I hope you like what you see."

"It's okay." By the way my nipples have hardened and the twisting in my core, I know that what I see is much, much better than okay.

He turns, giving me a great view of his tight ass and locks the bathroom door before walking toward me. I hurry and rinse the shampoo from my hair. When I open my eyes, Ricky is inside the shower, close enough to touch.

"I guess we fit," I say.

"Maybe we should work to conserve space?" Reaching out, he splays his fingers over my hips and pulls me closer.

I tip my chin upward, keeping my gaze locked with his. "Riverbend hasn't imploded with news of our dating. Devan and Justin may, if they hear us in here."

Ricky runs the pad of his thumb over my lower lip. "Last night, you were sleeping with your lips slightly parted."

"Don't you dare say I was snoring."

His cheeks rise. "I was going to say, it took all my self-restraint not to kiss you."

Leaning into his chest, I hum. "You can kiss me now."

And kiss me, he does.

I feel a cosmic connection as our lips touch and the spray rains warm water over our bodies. Sparks ignite throughout my heated bloodstream as our tongues join the dance. I lift my hands to his broad shoulders, the shampoo residue on my fingers making a slick interface as I slide my touch over his muscles.

Ricky, too, utilizes the Braille method as his hands wander over my flesh. Inch by inch, we study each other, feeling our way over each curve and investigating each crevice. My breathing hitches as he slides two long fingers inside me.

Aware of our surroundings, I bite down on his

shoulder, stifling a cry as he curls his fingers, moving in and out of me. As if he's found the switch to ignite my entire body, I tense, his ministrations setting off detonations far from the epicenter. Pressing up on my toes, I try to ease the pressure, while at the same time wanting it to keep building.

He lowers his lips to my breasts, tugging on each nipple with his teeth in a painful and pleasureful way. His erection probes my stomach, making its needs known. With the constant spray of the shower and the fireworks exploding within me, I'm on sensory overload as I swallow my sounds of ecstasy.

After catching my breath, I fall to my knees, careful of the slippery surface, finding myself level with his hardened cock.

"Fuck, Marilyn," he growls.

"Your turn to try to stay quiet."

"Shit," he mutters as I stick out my tongue and lap the crown.

My thumb and fingers don't touch as I grasp his girth, feeling the soft surface covering the rock-hard rod.

Ricky widens his stance while reaching for the tile wall.

Opening my mouth as wide as I can, I take only the tip, closing my lips and swirling my tongue over the mushroom crown. Backing down, I slide back up, each time taking more and more, until he's teasing the back of my throat. I hold the root, giving him pleasure with both my hands and my mouth. It's as I roll his balls between my fingers that Ricky curses, his legs grow rigid, and his cock tightens. Stream after stream of warm come covers my tongue as I quickly swallow.

The small shower echoes with a "pop" as I pull my lips away. Still on my knees, I look up, taking in the statue of the man before me. Mythological gods pale in comparison to the male specimen under my spell.

Ricky swallows, his Adam's apple bobbing as he offers me his hand. "That was...perfect."

My knees twinge from the hard tub and my jaw throbs from being open, but as I look into his gaze, every ache is worth it. I'd do it again and again to see that level of admiration. With his hand behind my neck, he takes my mouth, bruising my lips as he claims what I've wanted him to claim for as long as I can remember.

By the time we wash each other, I'm unsure of how long we've been in the shower. Devan is right; the water stayed warm.

With a towel wrapped around my breasts and another wrapped around Ricky's waist, we stand side by side at the vanity. I'm combing out my long hair as he's trimming his facial hair.

His gaze meets mine in the mirror. "We should have driven together."

"Now," I say with a chuckle. "I hadn't planned on telling anyone."

"Because you don't trust me."

He doesn't say it as a question.

"I've decided to live in the here and now. Whether we have a week together or a lifetime, it's more than I ever dared to hope for."

Ricky turns and cups my cheek. "I'm not making promises I won't keep, but I know I want more than a week."

"Living in the here and now."

We both jump at the knock on the door and break out in laughter.

"Yes?" I call.

"Just making sure you're both alive."

I open the door at the sound of Devan's voice and peer at her through an open crack. "Alive and well."

Chapter Twenty-Two

Ricky

It's been almost two weeks since the partner dinner. I've had two meetings with Mr. Stevens, one on the phone and one in person. Today, I have my first solo in-person meeting with Mr. Parker.

While I don't have any news on the hiring front with Parker and Stevens, on a personal note, the last two weeks have been better than any two weeks in my memory. Marilyn and I are officially dating. I brought her to my apartment, and after she met Max, we agreed to spend our time at her place. I've only spent weekend nights, but I made sure to keep my end of the deal and cook her breakfast.

Today is Thursday, and since we didn't see each

other last night and I'm early for my meeting with Mr. Parker, I make a detour.

Instead of heading to Mr. Parker's office, I find my way to the third floor, to the reception desk where I dropped off the letter to Marilyn two weeks ago.

"Is Ms. James in?" I ask the receptionist.

The woman's lips curl as she sizes me up and down. "You're the one who left her the letter."

"Guilty."

"Your name?"

"Richard Dunn."

"Just a minute."

I wait as she pushes some buttons and speaks into her headset. After a few moments, she removes the headset. "Follow me to Ms. James's office."

The receptionist leads me through a closed door to a hallway of doors. She knocks lightly on one. Next to the door is the nameplate: *Marilyn James, Wealth Adviser*.

"Come in," Marilyn calls. She stands from behind the glass desk.

I can't help but scan from her rich chestnut hair down her figure. Even in the blouse, jacket, and skirt, I see each of her curves, imagining the way they look without the clothes.

Marilyn smiles. "Thank you, Klara."

Klara, the receptionist, nods and leaves the two of us alone.

"I didn't expect you to visit me," she says, walking around the desk and dusting off the lapels of my new suit coat. "You look very handsome."

We share a chaste kiss.

"And you're stunning." I turn a full circle, taking in the bookcases, chairs, and window. "Wow, you have a window."

Marilyn laughs. "A little bigger than a porthole on a ship, but it's glass."

She's exaggerating. While it isn't a floor-to-ceiling window, it's a normal-sized view of the outside. I've learned from her stories that, as an intern, she was in a cubicle, surrounded by other cubicles.

"I'm glad you like the suit. You picked it out."

"You're going on your second in-person interview with the partners. I thought it was time you move up from the one suit."

"Hey, that suit has served me well. I've had it since my grandpa's funeral." I try to think. "That's six years ago."

Marilyn nods, her lips pressed together in a tight smile. "You deserve a new suit."

"I hate to use you as a spy," I preface. "Have you heard anything about the hires for the new position?"

Marilyn's smile fades. "I heard something this morning."

Shit.

"I don't like your expression."

"The talent acquisition team agreed on hiring six of the twenty applicants from the dinner."

"When are they going to let us know?"

She reaches for my hand. "They already have. Calls went out yesterday. The other applicants will be notified by snail mail."

Gritting my teeth, I exhale. "Then why the fuck am I here?"

"I don't know for sure, but I believe the partners are interested in you for research and development with the agriculture wealth campaign." She brightens her smile. "This is much bigger than the position you interviewed for, Ricky. This is moving up."

"Do you know that for sure?"

Marilyn shakes her head. "I'm reading tea leaves, but why would Mr. Parker schedule this meeting if you're going to get a Dear John letter?"

I sit down in one of the chairs opposite Marilyn's desk. "Maybe this isn't the world for me."

She crosses her arms over her breasts, leans against her desk, and gives me her best scowl. "You are not allowed to give up, Richard Dunn. First, the doors here haven't closed. You're meeting with the second of two partners in a week. And second, the world of finance is not all contained within Parker and Stevens. You have other options. Didn't you say that your headhunter messaged you about a position with Chase?"

I nod. "I had my heart set on here."

Marilyn crouches down next to the chair. For only a brief second, I have visions of her on her knees at Devan's house, in the shower…

Her voice pulls me back to reality.

"Ricky, walk into Mr. Parker's office with the confidence of bringing more to the table than any of the other applicants. They were hired to do menial and brain-numbing tasks. I know. I did those tasks as an intern. The other applicants went from high school straight into college. Their life experiences are social media, gaming, and partying. You've had a life and career."

"It wasn't—"

I'm mesmerized by the determination in her voice and the conviction in her blue stare.

"It was a career," Marilyn argues. "Ask Justin. While my dad didn't farm, I grew up watching your dad, you, and others work your asses off. The people hired for the starting positions don't know the meaning of a hard day's work. You do. Take that into your meeting with Mr. Parker."

"Are you my cheerleader?"

Marilyn stands and brushes her skirt. "I have news for you, Mr. Dunn, I don't give false praise. It's a waste of breath. I listened to you at the partner dinner, and we've talked. You deserve a cheerleader."

"And a new suit."

Marilyn lifts an eyebrow. "Maybe more. Go have a great meeting, and then we can talk about what else you deserve."

My lips curl. "Maybe coming here first wasn't a good idea."

"Why?"

"Because I don't want the impression I make on Mr. Parker to be walking into his office with a hard-on."

"It is impressive."

Shaking my head, I stand, reach for her hands, and lean forward, kissing her nose. "Thank you. When you're not being sassy, you know exactly what to say."

"I can be sassy."

"I know you can."

"Come to my place for dinner tonight?"

I nod, my thoughts going to Mr. Parker and the knowledge that all the positions have been filled. As I'm headed toward the receptionist's desk, I notice the man walking my direction is Marilyn's ex. It's one of those moments when I can't decide if I should acknowledge him or just let him pass by.

"Dunn," he says, looking me up and down. "What are you doing here?"

"Perkins, nice to see you again."

"Maybe you haven't heard, but the positions have already been filled."

I straighten my shoulders. "I've been informed. I'm here for a meeting with Mr. Parker about another position." I don't know if that's one hundred percent accurate, but I'm going with it.

Bryce's eyes narrow. "What other position? I'm on the talent acquisition team."

Shrugging, I force a smile. "That sounds like a question for one of the partners. I've had two meetings with Mr. Stevens."

"You're on the wrong floor."

"Thanks for the information. I need to get to my meeting." I don't wait for him to say goodbye or end our conversation. I'm perfectly content with where it concluded. As I reach for the handle of the door to the reception area, I notice Bryce stepping into Marilyn's office.

I tell myself not to think about that. She's a capable woman, and I know she isn't interested in Bryce, even if he is interested in her. Suddenly, I wonder if my not getting one of the positions is courtesy of Mr. Bryce Talent Acquisition Team Perkins.

"Richard Dunn, for Mr. Parker," I say to a different receptionist on the top floor.

"Please have a seat, Mr. Dunn. Mr. Parker is on a call, but he'll be with you shortly."

Chapter Twenty-Three

Marilyn

The lemon chicken is in the oven. A fresh, leafy salad is chilling in the refrigerator. The rice is in the pressure cooker, ready for me to hit the button. I even have a bottle of white zinfandel waiting to be uncorked. The only thing missing from our dinner is Ricky.

I expected him to come back to my office after his meeting with Mr. Parker. When he didn't, I checked my cell phone for missed calls or messages. By the time I was leaving work, I sent him a text message, asking about the meeting and reminding him about dinner at my place.

Now it's a quarter to seven and, still, no word.

In the bedroom, I check my reflection. After

work, I came home, changed clothes, and freshened up. All the while, my talk with Bryce replays in my head.

After Ricky left my office, Bryce appeared.

Looking up, I smile, expecting to see Ricky back in my doorway for one more pep talk. My smile fades at the sight of Bryce Perkins. Even in his business casual attire, he doesn't hold a candle to Ricky. His torso doesn't slim down to a V, accentuating his shoulders. I don't even want to compare their facial features. "Do you need something?" I ask.

Bryce comes in the door and takes a seat opposite my desk, leaning back and crossing one ankle over his knee. "I thought I'd tell you personally that your friend—or was he a date?" He shrugs. "Anyway, Dick Dunn isn't Parker and Stevens material."

I feel my blood pressure rise as I clench my jaw. "I think you mean that he isn't entry-level material."

"No. I said what I mean. He's not working here." Bryce lowers his leg to the floor and leans forward. "Marilyn, I'm sure it's hard to hear the truth, especially from me."

"And what truth would that be?"

"He was just using you to get a job here. Honestly, it was painfully obvious to everyone else."

I recall what Ricky said, that he thought Bryce was still into me. "His name is Rich," I correct. "And my relationship with him is none of your business, just as your relationship with Beth is none of mine."

Bryce shrugs. "I'm afraid Beth and I agreed to part ways. She isn't like you. Too high-maintenance for my liking."

A scoff escapes my throat. "Two high-maintenance people in a relationship would be exhausting."

He placates me with a soft laugh. "I spoke with Rich*"—he emphasizes the name— "in the hallway. You know, some people aren't meant for the white-collar world." He lifts his hands. "There's nothing wrong with manual labor. Lord knows we need those people."*

Those people.

His condescending tone grates on my nerves. "Bryce, do you want something, because I have a meeting with one of my clients in a few minutes, and I need to review their portfolio."

"I came to ask you to dinner, a real one. Just you and me."

I shake my head. "Maybe you've forgotten, but there's no you and me. We're done."

"I haven't forgotten. I'm hoping you can see a way to give us another chance."

My temples begin to throb. "There's no us.*"*

"Marilyn, seeing you with someone else...it made me realize. We're kindred spirits. We've both tasted success and have the thirst for more. I knew that about you

when you were an intern. Your drive, ability, and willingness to learn drew me to you. Together, you and I could be a power couple in the wealth management world."

Inhaling, I stand. "I'm not interested."

He also stands and scrunches his lips. "Oh, do you think you're in a relationship with him?"

I know I am.

Instead of saying that, I once again tell Bryce to leave my office.

He walks to the door. "I've missed you, Marilyn. Have your fun, but when he breaks your heart, I want you to know that I'll be here to help you put it back together."

"Bye, Bryce."

Even now, hours later, the whole conversation has me steaming. I can't help but think that the reason Ricky wasn't chosen for one of the positions is Bryce. Of course, I can't prove that. And with each passing minute, I worry that Bryce is right about Ricky.

Was he using me?

I find my phone and try calling Ricky. Biting my lip, I wait. The call goes to voice mail, just like all the calls I've made since seeing him this afternoon. As I'm about to put down my phone, it vibrates with an incoming call. The screen says Devan.

While I'm happy to talk to my friend, I'm disappointed that it's not Ricky. After pushing the green icon, I answer, "Hi, Dev."

"Marilyn."

It is Ricky.

"What's the matter?" I ask, wondering why he's calling me on Devan's phone. My pulse increases. "Is Devan all right?"

"Devan is fine." He takes a deep breath. "It's Justin. There's been an accident."

I fall into a nearby chair, my blood draining to my feet. "What kind of accident?"

"He's hurt. Dad called me as I was getting out of the meeting with Herold Parker. I hurried to my apartment and packed a few things. Now I'm in Bloomington. Justin's in surgery."

"I thought your parents were in Florida."

"They are. Devan called them."

My emotions are all over the place, sad about Justin and relieved that Bryce wasn't right. "I've been calling you."

"Marilyn, I'm sorry. I have no fucking idea where my phone is. It's probably in my apartment. I wasn't thinking straight."

"There's no reason to apologize. Will Justin be okay?"

"Fucking hope so. He was working on some machinery, and it fell, crushing one of his legs."

I gasp. "Oh no. How is Devan?"

"Upset, but strong."

I do some mental math on time and distance. "Which Bloomington hospital? I can be there in less than an hour." Our dinner no longer matters.

"You don't have to. It's dark."

His concern makes me smile. "I'm on my way. My car has these things called headlights. Wonderful invention for driving in the dark."

"IU Health. Check in at the front desk and call Devan's phone. I'll come get you. This place is a maze."

"Ricky?"

"Yeah?"

"How did your meeting with Mr. Parker go?"

"I'll tell you all about it when you get here."

I wrinkle my nose. "Is it bad?"

"No," he answers quickly. "I think it's good."

I let out a long breath. "Tell Devan I'm on my way."

My next call is to Jill. Ten minutes later, I'm getting into the back seat of Todd's SUV. Once I'm settled, I look up to the front seat. "Todd, you didn't have to come."

"I'm not a fan of the two of you taking off in the dark on country roads." He reaches across and lays his hand on Jill's knee. "I don't want anything to happen to you."

Jill turns in my direction as Todd starts to drive. "Besides, we figured if you didn't want to come back with us, Ricky might be able to give you a ride." Her expression saddens. "Have you heard anything more about Justin?"

I shake my head. "Just what I told you." I fight back tears. "We were just with them two weeks ago."

Jill nods. "I know. And we made the guys leave."

"They didn't mind," I say, recalling the breakfast the next morning. "They had a good time at Decoy Ducks."

A little over an hour later, Todd finds a space to park in the visitor parking lot, and the three of us stuff our hands into our coat pockets and trudge forward through the icy air. By the time we reach the door, my ears are prickling with the cold.

It's as we enter that I see the people checking in, showing their IDs for entrance.

Chapter Twenty-Four

Marilyn

"Kandace," I call as she and her husband, Dax, walk toward the elevators.

Kandace Richards, Justin's sister, turns. She's easy to spot with her bright auburn hair. Her eyes are puffy from crying. Seeing our group, she asks, "Are you here for Justin?"

I nod, wanting to get to her but needing to follow hospital procedures. "We are. Do you know where you're going?"

"Surgery waiting room," Dax says. "Second floor."

"We'll be up soon," Todd says.

Jill leans into her husband and looks at me. "I'm surprised they weren't already here."

"I suppose they needed someone to watch the girls."

"Oh, that kid thing," she says with a half smile.

It's nearly nine o'clock by the time we make it to the second floor. The first waiting room we come to is filled with people I've known all my life. Justin and Ricky's friends were always older, but that doesn't stop people from knowing one another. Scanning the group, I look for Devan.

She's seated next to Bridget Sheers, Justin's mom.

Todd stops to talk to a man from Riverbend I recognize, although his name is escaping me. Jill and I rush Devan's direction, weaving through the sea of people.

When Devan sees us, her eyes fill with tears as she stands. Jill and I both wrap her in our arms. "How is he?" I ask.

Devan wipes her nose with the back of her hand. "We've only had one update since he went into surgery."

"Can you tell us what happened?" Jill asks.

Devan turns toward her mother-in-law.

"Go and talk to your friends," Bridget says. "Stay close." She forces a smile. "I'm sure we'll hear more soon."

"Mrs. Sheers," I say. "I'm so sorry."

She reaches for my hand. "Thank you, Marilyn. How are you liking Indianapolis?"

I'm a bit surprised she knows that much about me. "I'm liking it better lately."

Mrs. Sheers grins. "Devan was telling me." She looks around. "Ricky is here somewhere."

"Right now, I'm more concerned with Devan."

"Thank you" —Mrs. Sheers turns to Jill— "and to you for making the trip. Friends we can count on are the most important."

With Devan between us, Jill and I lead her to a small room with a coffeepot, a rack of snacks, and a table with four chairs.

Once we're seated, Devan starts talking. "I don't know for sure how long he was there—out in the barn. When I got home from school, I couldn't find him and assumed he was working. It was weird because I hadn't heard from him since after lunch. Usually, he sends me silly text messages during the day."

"You found him?" Jill asks.

Devan nods as more tears slide down her cheeks. "I've never been more scared. I couldn't wake him." I wrap my arm around her shoulders. "His phone was in the pocket of the leg that was under the baler. It's shattered. He couldn't have called for help if he was awake. I just don't know..."

I shake my head. "I don't know much about farm equipment. Is the baler big?"

"About 23,000 pounds."

"What happened?" I ask.

"I think he had it jacked up to work underneath, and something fell."

"Have the doctors told you anything?" Jill asks.

"They think they can save his leg." When our eyes open wide, Devan says, "I don't understand it all, but there was fear with something like this that the leg loses blood supply. As bad as it was, I guess it could be worse."

"How long has he been in surgery?" I ask.

Devan looks at her watch. "They finally took him back around four thirty."

I cover Devan's hand, and Jill lays hers over ours. "He's going to be all right."

"We just started our lives together. I can't lose him." Devan's voice cracks.

I blink away new tears. "You won't lose him. Justin Sheers has always been hardheaded and stubborn. That man isn't about to leave you."

"Devan?"

We all look toward the deep voice. My breathing hitches as I take in Ricky. He looks totally different than he did hours ago in my office. His new suit has been replaced by jeans, a thermal, and an unbuttoned flannel shirt. His shiny loafers are gone, hiking boots in their place. However, it's his expression that is the biggest contrast. In the course of hours, Ricky looks as if he's taken on the weight of the world.

Ricky walks into the small kitchenette. "Dr. Evans is out there. She wants to give an update, but she won't until you're with us."

Devan nods, grabbing a napkin from the counter, and she wipes her tears. Ricky waits for me as Jill takes Devan's hand, and they walk ahead of us.

Ricky wraps an arm around me and kisses the top of my head. "Thank you for being here for Devan."

"I'm here for you too."

Pressing his lips together, he nods. "Let's go hear what the doctor has to say."

As we join the others in the larger waiting room, a woman in scrubs is talking. Devan is standing next to Bridget, their hands clasped and fingers interlocked. Justin's dad, Randy, is standing at his wife's side. Everyone else is standing—Kandace, Dax, Todd, and more of Justin's friends, Galvin, Cory, Harvey, and Nick.

"...through the first stage of the surgery..."

I hold tight to Ricky's arm.

She continues. "Often in cases such as this, there can be severe damage to muscles, tissues, and circulation. The good news is that by a miracle, Justin's circulation wasn't impeded. His leg never lost blood flow. Repairing the muscles, nerves, and bone is time-consuming. He will probably be in surgery for another five hours."

The whole room makes a collective gasp.

"I didn't want you to worry, Mrs. Sheers." She's talking to Devan. "Your husband has made it through the hardest part. I wouldn't say we're out of the woods, but you can breathe a sigh of relief."

"Thank you, Dr. Evans," Devan says.

As soon as Dr. Evans walks away, everyone surrounds Devan. She lifts her hands. "Thank you all for being here. I don't think you want to stay another five hours. I promise to let you know as soon as he's out of surgery."

While everyone nods, no one leaves. Quietly, all those around us take a seat.

Ricky looks down at me and smiles. "This is Riverbend."

I swallow the lump in my throat. "It makes you wonder why we want to leave."

Tugging my hand, he says, "Come with me. We need to talk." He calls across to his sister and parents, "We're not leaving. We'll be back."

I'm thinking about what he said—we need to talk. *Has there ever been a more daunting sentence?*

I brace myself for what Bryce said, for Ricky to

break up with me because he didn't get the job at Parker and Stevens. It's selfish of me to be thinking about us instead of Justin, but Bryce's warning upset me more than I realized. And then when Ricky didn't call or show...

We're quiet as we make our way down the hallways. At this time of night, few people are about. We spot a bench near a window. Beyond the glass, the sky is black. Lights down below in the parking lot shine as leafless trees and bushes sway in the wind.

"I'm sorry I didn't call you sooner," he says, still holding my hand.

"It's all right. You didn't have your phone, and your mind was on Justin."

He inhales and nods.

"How did today's meeting go?" I ask.

Ricky inhales and sits taller. "Very well. Mr. Parker offered me a job."

It's the best news I've heard in a while. My neck stiffens, and I open my eyes wide. "That's great news."

"I thought so too. Before my dad's call, I couldn't wait to tell you." He drops my hand, spreads his knees, and leans back. His tone lacks the excitement I would have expected. "I'm supposed to meet with HR tomorrow and go through the paperwork. Mr. Parker said they'd have all the information about salary and benefits."

"Why don't you sound happier?"

Ricky rolls his eyes and stares up at the ceiling. "Randy and Justin have over a thousand acres of land to farm. Randy isn't in the best of health. No one is talking about tomorrow, but there's no way Justin will be able to do what he normally does this spring. Randy and Bridget were talking about Justin's recovery time. They're talking months, not weeks."

"You're going to put your dream on hold for your friend?"

Plopping his elbows on his knees, Ricky leans forward, cradling his forehead. "Farming is about making enough money to get to the next year." He stands up, moving back and forth like a caged animal. "The agricultural wealth Mr. Parker is talking about is for maybe five percent of Indiana farmers. Hell, five percent nationwide of family-owned farms. The real wealth is in conglomerates. If Justin can't get his fields ready, plant his crop, and maintain it, there won't be a crop to harvest in the fall. That harvest pays for the next year." He sighs. "They'll lose the farm, not just the Dunn part but the Sheers's farm as well."

"You want to move back to Riverbend?"

Ricky rubs his palms over his beard growth. "Fuck. No and yes." He points to the waiting room. "If I was in a car accident in Indy, there might be two people in the waiting room. Justin has half the town."

I scoff. "It's not half the town, and I think you'd have more than two people." I stand, meeting him chest-to-chest and lean toward him. "You'd have me."

"Even if I decide to tell Mr. Parker no?"

I take a step back, shocked by his question. "You would tell him no?"

Ricky stares at me, unblinking. "I can't do both."

I'm not sure if my disappointment is for Ricky or for me. Maybe it's for both of us. "Please don't make a rash decision."

"What's the matter, Marilyn? You don't want to date a farmer from Riverbend?"

"I never said that. You said that about me."

Ricky wraps his arms around my waist, looking down at me, and exhales. "I can't take the GMAT with all that's happening. I can look for a job in the fall when Justin is well. I've got money from the sale of the farm I've been stashing away. I can survive without this job. Justin's farm won't."

"I wonder if there's a compromise."

"What kind of compromise?"

"Parker and Stevens wants you because" —I lay my hand over his chest— "you have a farmer's heart" —I move my finger to his temple— "and a farmer's knowledge. They don't have applicants with your skill set every day. Tell them what happened. Be completely honest with them." I tilt my head. "You have your dream in front of you, ready for the taking, and yet you're willing to give it up so Justin can keep his dream. Maybe the partners will come up with a solution."

"I can't ask them to do that."

"Yes, you can. And what about those other men in there?" I tilt my head toward the waiting room. "Don't you think they are all thinking similar things?"

"Justin doesn't work their family farm."

"No, but they're Riverbend born and bred. They're all thinking about how they can help. Doesn't Kandace's husband help on weekends?"

Ricky nods. "It's not their responsibility."

"I admire your dedication, but Ricky, it's not yours either." I lift myself up on my tiptoes and brush my lips with his. Despite his nonresponse, I say, "I support your decision."

Hand in hand, we walk toward the larger waiting room. Before we turn the corner, we hear the commotion.

Chapter Twenty-Five

Ricky

"Mom and Dad," I say, dropping Marilyn's hand and giving them each a hug. "How did you get here so fast?"

"We found a direct flight to Indy and rented a car," Mom says, looking around and spotting Devan. Tears coat Mom's cheeks as she and my sister embrace. Holding Devan against her shoulder, Mom pets Devan's hair. "He's going to be all right." Mom nods. "I've claimed it."

The room buzzes with discussions as Mom and Dad join the conversations. Bridget gives Mom an update as Dad talks to Randy. For a few minutes, I stand, leaning against the wall, my arms crossed over my chest, accepting my own decisions. I can walk away from my job at the mall. If I never sell another pair of basketball shoes, I'll be content.

It's walking away from Marilyn that bothers me, even more than turning down the job at Parker and Stevens. That firm may be my dream, but in only a few weeks, I saw Marilyn as more than a dream. I saw her as my future. I saw us as a future.

This decision is going to do what I swore not to do.

It's going to hurt Marilyn—again.

This time, like last time, it's for her own good. Except, unlike last time, I know what I'm doing. That doesn't mean I don't hate it, but it means it's the right thing to do. She says she supports my decision, but her suggestion of a compromise tells me that deep down, she wants me to take the job.

Looking around, I spot Marilyn sitting next to Jill. As I do, my mom appears at my side, her arm latching through mine.

"Are you going to formally introduce us?"

My eyes open wide.

"Or are you not serious with her?"

"How do you even know about Marilyn?"

Mom presses her lips together. "Well, let's see... your sister, for one. And then there is Betty Kolberg.

Oh, and Joyce from the diner. I've also known Marilyn all her life."

Closing my eyes, I shake my head. "You were in Florida."

"I had my phone." She lowers her voice. "Are the rumors wrong?"

My lips curl. "No, Mom. They're right."

"Then what's wrong?"

"Justin is what's wrong."

Mom pulls me out into the hallway. "Honey, he'll get better."

I lift my chin toward Marilyn. "Look at her. She's beautiful and so damn smart. We're interested in the same things. She knows what she wants and has worked hard for it."

"She sounds like a wonderful woman."

"She is," I admit.

"Then tell me what's wrong."

I inhale. "Marilyn doesn't deserve to be with someone stuck in Riverbend. She deserves someone who lives where she wants to live, someone who doesn't have dirt permanently under his fingernails."

"You left Riverbend."

I exhale, my nostrils flaring. "I got a job offer today."

Mom's eyes open wide. "You did? That's fantastic."

I nod. "It's with the firm I really wanted." I turn and look into my mom's eyes. "I applied for an entry level, but that wasn't what they offered me."

"I'm so proud of you."

"I'm going to turn it down."

Mom's lips gape open. "Richard John, tell me why."

"Because I'm not going to let Justin lose the farm."

"That's very noble of you, but I don't—"

"Stop, please, Mom." I work to not raise my voice. "We may have sold the farm to Justin and Devan, but I can't turn my back now. He'll need help. Hell, I graduated a semester early. I can look for a job after this year's crop is harvested."

"What about Marilyn?" Mom asks.

As a lump forms in the back of my throat, I look over at her. She says she will support me, no matter my decision, but I can't do that to her. I'm not dragging her back to Riverbend. "I don't know," I reply.

"Ricky, don't make life-changing decisions when everything is in chaos. Devan told me how happy you two were the other weekend."

"Marilyn deserves better."

"Shouldn't that be her decision?"

I lift my hand, point at Marilyn, and curl my finger, beckoning her to us.

Her blue eyes open wide as she looks around in all

directions before gesturing to herself. "Me?" she mouths.

I nod, unable to hold back my grin.

Damn, it's painful watching her come toward us, knowing that soon I won't be holding her in my arms. Tonight was supposed to be our celebration. I push those thoughts away as she comes closer. Once she's standing before us, I say, "I know you know each other, but Marilyn, this is Mom. Mom, this is Marilyn."

My mother smiles. "I've only known Marilyn since she and Devan were in the same Sunday school class, wearing diapers."

Marilyn's cheeks glow with a rosy hue. "Janet, it's good to see you."

Mom pulls Marilyn into a hug and whispers something in her ear. As Marilyn pulls away, she nods and smiles.

"Are you going to tell me what you're saying?" I ask.

"No," both ladies say at the same time.

Marilyn reaches for my hand, but I pull it back.

"Um," Marilyn says. "Todd and Jill are headed back to Carmel. I've decided to email my supervisor and let them know I won't be in tomorrow. I can stay overnight, at least."

"Don't do that."

"I want to stay, for Devan and for you."

I shake my head. "Devan has all of fucking Riverbend."

Her eyes widen. "Then for you."

"You have a job, an important job. Devan will understand. Besides, you can come back on the weekend, and hopefully, Justin will be up for visitors."

Marilyn swallows. I sense her feeling me pulling away. The thing she doesn't understand is that it's killing me.

"Okay," she says. "I guess I'll go back with them."

Mom reaches for Marilyn's hand. "Honey, it's good to see you."

She gives my mom a half smile. "Take care of Devan."

"We will."

I turn to Mom. "Can I stay at your place in town, or do you think I should stay out with Devan?"

"Why don't you ask your sister?"

"I'll do that." I nod to Marilyn. "See you later."

"Bye," Marilyn says, turning away.

I can't watch her leave. Instead, I look for my sister.

Chapter Twenty-Six

Marilyn

After hugging Devan and asking her to keep me updated, no matter the time of day or night, I look around the waiting room. Ricky said he was going to ask Devan where he should stay, but he's nowhere to be found.

Jill bumps my shoulder. "Are you sure you want to go back?"

Swallowing, I nod.

I can't quell the feeling of sadness that's come over me. I tell myself it is about Justin and for Devan, but I know it's Ricky. There was something in his voice that makes me uneasy.

"Are you going to say goodbye to Ricky?" Jill asks.

Pressing my lips together, I shake my head. "We already said bye. I don't know where he is."

Settling in Todd and Jill's back seat, I pull out my phone, ready to send Ricky a text message, when I remember that he doesn't have his phone. With a sigh, I push my phone back into my purse. Our ride is relatively quiet. There isn't a lot to say when one of your friends is hurt and another is hurting.

"Todd?" I ask. His gaze goes to the rearview mirror. "I know you weren't really part of the farming in Riverbend."

"Not willingly," he says with a scoff. "As a teenager, my dad made me help at the Gordons' farm. I think everyone in town did their time there."

"Mrs. Gordon is still keeping it going," Jill says. "She has to be a hundred if she's fifty."

I laugh. "Jack is over fifty, and I've heard him talk about working that farm as a kid."

"Yep. She's a hundred," Jill says. "Why are you asking?"

"Ricky was talking about Justin's recovery and how he'll need help."

"He won't ask for it," Todd volunteers. "Justin Sheers has always been stubborn."

I laugh. "That seems to be the general accepted description. But he will need help. Do you think he could hire someone?"

"Randy will do what he can," Todd says. "And Dax will help when he can."

"Will that be enough?"

"Probably not," Todd says, telling me what I already know. "It sucks. Justin took on a lot of work, combining the two farms. If he only had half the acres, but damn, I think there's about a thousand."

That was what Ricky said.

I lay my head back on the seat and watch the world pass by the SUV windows, feeling like every mile that I go is a mile away from Ricky that I'll never get back. Closing my eyes, I send good thoughts to Devan, hoping the surgeon comes out with favorable news.

"Marilyn."

Jill's voice comes to me in my dream seconds before I realize she's waking me. I startle awake, seeing that we're parked in front of my apartment building.

"Sorry," I say. "I fell asleep."

"You were both sleeping," Todd says. "And I'm not going to say which one of you was snoring."

"I don't snore," Jill and I say in unison.

She gets out of the car and gives me a hug. "If you hear anything..."

I nod. "If you do."

Climbing the steps to my second-floor apartment, I wish above anything that I had a way to communicate with Ricky. For the first time in years, I yearn for a house phone. If I knew which house he was staying at. Inside my apartment, I see that it's after midnight.

Is Justin out of surgery?

By the time I'm ready for bed, I still don't have any new messages on my phone. I send Devan a heart emoji and turn in for the night. In the morning, I wake to multiple text messages from Devan.

The first one is time stamped after 1:00 a.m.

Justin is out of surgery.

The next one is time stamped just before 3:00 a.m.

They finally have him in a room.

At 5:25 a.m., just before my alarm, I receive the third message.

He's awake.

There are tears in my eyes as I send her a response.

. . .

Give him a hug for me. I love you both. Get some sleep.

On my way to work, I swing by Ricky's apartment. From all his stories about his roommate, I'm not exactly sure who will answer the door, if anyone. It's nearly seven thirty when I knock on the door. I wait. I knock again. I wait.

I'm about to walk away when the door opens.

Max's blond hair is in disarray, and he's wearing only a pair of boxer shorts, not briefs. I try to keep my line of sight to his eyes. The fly on the boxers doesn't seem to fasten.

"Um," I say, "Ricky lost his phone, and I wanted to come by and see if it's here."

Max rubs his eyes. "Yeah, you can come in." He opens the door wider.

I step inside. The living room has two open pizza boxes with nothing but crumbs. And a video game is on the TV screen. I can't see into Max's room, but it doesn't appear as if he has company.

"Have you seen his phone?"

Max yawns and points to the kitchen. "I think that's his in there."

The kitchen is as clean as the living room, which

isn't a compliment. On the table by a box of cereal is a black iPhone. I pick it up. "I think it's his." I swipe the screen, and nothing happens. The phone is dead.

"I don't know," Max says with a shrug. "Where is Rich?"

"He's down in Riverbend. A friend was injured yesterday."

"Oh man." He walks to the coffeepot and lifts the carafe. "Want some coffee? I'm not sure when this was made." He looks at me with wide eyes. "Coffee doesn't go bad, does it?"

"Could the phone belong to anyone else?" I ask.

Max contemplates the question for what seems longer than necessary. "I don't think so." He wrinkles his forehead. "I don't remember anyone being here last night." He pours the coffee into a mug from the sink. "I haven't gotten any messages. I didn't know."

"Well—" I lift the phone. "—he doesn't have this, so it's hard for him to message."

Max laughs. "Yeah. I like you. You're the best girlfriend he's brought around."

"The best?"

"The only," Max says, lowering his voice as if he's telling me a secret.

"Do you know where his charger is?"

"Probably his bedroom."

Carrying the phone, I make my way down the hall to where I know Ricky's bedroom is. It feels a little like snooping, and I don't want to be that kind of girlfriend. Turning the knob, I push the door open.

The last time I was at his apartment, Ricky's bedroom was neat. Today, his new suit is lying on the floor, along with the dress shirt and tie. Drawers are open and items are hanging out.

"He left in a hurry," I say to myself as I bend down and pick up his suit. There's no sense having it wrinkled. I smooth the fabric before hanging the pants and suit coat on hangers in his closet.

Remembering my task at hand, I look around for his charger. It isn't on his bedside stand, so I check his desk. The first thing I see is a spiral notebook. Peering toward the door to see if Max is watching, I open the notebook. Before I can read his words, I chastise myself for snooping.

That condemnation only lasts a millisecond, before I see what Ricky wrote. It's about his meetings with people from Parker and Stevens. Each entry is dated all the way back through last September, when he first decided to apply for a job.

I sit on the side of his bed and quickly read his entries.

With each one, my heartstrings are pulled. He

mentions how much he wants to work at a reputable firm. He knows more about the history of Parker and Stevens than I do. I flip the pages until I get to the dinner two weeks ago.

Friday, January …

I was dreading the dinner after what happened last night. To be clear with myself when I read this later, I didn't write this entry until Sunday night, after the dinner. Let me say, Friday night exceeded all my expectations. To my honor and shock, Marilyn James kept her word. I didn't think she wasn't a person who kept her word, I just didn't think I deserved for her to show. She did!

I met Ralph Stevens, and we talked about farming. His grandfather owned a five-hundred-acre farm in southern Michigan, and he has always had respect for the profession. He's asked me to speak to him on the phone on Monday. I also met Herold Parker. He's younger than Mr. Stevens and very interesting. I'd read that, originally, Herold's father had partnered with Ralph at Parker and Stevens. After the father died unexpectedly from an aneurysm, Herold Jr. went into business with Ralph Stevens. Marilyn introduced me to everyone in the room. It felt unreal that I, a nobody from Riverbend, was at that level. Cinderella at the ball and my Prince Charming was the most beautiful woman at the dinner. Maybe I can deserve Marilyn. I sure as hell am going to try.

I close the notebook, not wanting to read more.

"Did you find the charger?" Max asks, peeking into the room.

Laying the notebook back on the desk, I see the white cord and plug. "I found it." I hurriedly take the charger and stuff it into my purse. "I'm headed back down to Riverbend after work. I'll take this to Ricky."

Max laughs. "You're the only one who calls him that. It sounds like some name from a comic strip."

I can't come up with a Ricky in a comic strip. Richie Rich is my only connection. "It's the name he went by back in our hometown."

"You're from Riverbend too?"

"I am."

"Bet you're glad you're out of there."

"Not always." I pass by Max and head toward the front door. "Thanks for letting me in."

"I have to be at the mall at nine thirty. You saved me from being late."

"I need to get to work too." I open the door to their apartment. Max shuts it after I pass through.

My only thought is that Ricky deserves the job he

was offered. I learned more about Mr. Stevens and Mr. Parker in that one entry than I have learned in three years.

"Don't give up your dream," I say to myself as I make my way to my car.

Chapter Twenty-Seven

Marilyn

A watched pot never boils, my grandma used to say. Apparently, watching a clock also doesn't make time go any quicker. Thankfully, my last meeting of the day cancels, giving me the out I've been wanting, the out to head back to Riverbend—to Devan, Justin, and Ricky. I send Devan a quick text message and one to my mom, telling them both I'll be down in a few hours. I fill my mom in on what happened to Justin; however, seeing as she's in Riverbend, I would expect she already knows.

Texting Ricky is unnecessary since I have his phone. I've had it plugged in all day, and it's charged. The only thing keeping me from snooping is the face ID security and the fact that I don't want to be *that* girlfriend, the one who looks at his private things, like the notebook I accidentally read.

It wasn't exactly an accident, but that sounds better in my mind.

Gathering all my things, I make my way down to the front of the building, hoping to sneak out a little early without drawing too much attention. The elevator doors open on the first floor, and my hopes of an invisible escape are dashed.

"Marilyn," Mr. Stevens says, eyeing me up and down, no doubt assessing by my long coat and computer bag that I'm on my way out of the building.

"Mr. Stevens."

He tilts his head. "Are you in a hurry, or may we have a few minutes to speak?"

Like I could turn down one of the partners. "Of course I can take a few minutes."

He steps into the elevator and hits the button for the top floor.

We're quiet as the doors close. Finally, as we begin to ascend, I ask, "Is there a problem?"

"I'm hoping you can tell me." Small lines spider from the corners of his eyes as he lifts his face toward the ceiling and inhales. "Some days, I feel like I'm getting too old for all of this."

"Are you considering retirement?"

He scoffs. "Elenor doesn't want me at home

underfoot all day long." He grins. "I think she's hiding a male lover."

My eyes open wide.

"I'm teasing. She likes her space, and I respect that."

I let out a breath. "You could travel."

"I'm quite content with where we are." The doors open to his receptionists, and he gestures for me to exit first.

I step to the side, allowing him to lead the way as I follow him to his office.

"Please," he says once we're inside, "take off your coat. I have some questions that may, in the mind of some, be inappropriate."

I stop mid-unbuttoning my wool coat. "Excuse me?"

He has a tiredness about him that seems unfamiliar. His suit coat is gone, and his shirt is wrinkled. Mr. Stevens gestures toward the sofa and chairs in the corner of his office near the floor-to-ceiling windows.

Laying my coat over the back of one chair, I sit in the other and smooth my skirt over my legs. Never in all my time working at this firm has Mr. Stevens been inappropriate. If anything, he's always been kind and supportive.

Mr. Stevens takes a seat on the sofa, sitting forward, his knees spread. "Let me preface this with, it is perfectly acceptable for you to tell me that you don't know, you think it's wrong of me to ask you, or it's none of my business."

I inhale. "That's a bit foreboding."

"I received some surprising and sad news earlier today."

I wait, wondering if this is about Ricky and hoping it's not. Saying a prayer that Ricky listened to my advice and didn't make a rash decision. "What did you hear?"

He leans back, his nostrils flaring. "I heard from Mr. Dunn."

Closing my eyes, I inhale and tug on my lower lip. Mr. Stevens is looking at me as my eyes open.

"You know that he decided against accepting the position we offered him?"

"I know that working for Parker and Stevens has been his dream. I also know that Ricky...Rich is a good man with a strong work ethic. Also, like many men" —I smile— "sorry, but it's true, Rich thinks he needs to fix what's broken. He believes he's the only one capable, no matter the consequences."

"What broke?"

"What did Rich say to you?" I ask.

"This isn't a conversation we should be having."

"Probably not," I agree. "You're the one who asked me to your office."

Mr. Stevens nods. "He thanked us for the vote of confidence and said another opportunity has come up and he regretfully must decline our offer."

Swallowing, I make the decision to be completely honest and transparent. "Mr. Stevens, as you know, besides getting his associate's degree, Rich spent the first thirty-two years of his life working his family's farm."

Mr. Stevens nods.

"A few years ago, Jack Dunn, Rich's father, decided to sell the farm. There have been a few developers grabbing land when they can. Instead of going that route, the Dunns sold it to their daughter and son-in-law, who happens to own a neighboring farm. Altogether, Rich's friend, Justin, is now responsible for over a thousand acres of land. Rich and Justin have been best friends since they were toddlers." Not wanting to drag out the story too long, I jump to the issue at hand. "Yesterday, Justin Sheers was injured in an accident on that farm. He was working on a rather heavy piece of machinery, and somehow it fell, crushing his femur. We were all at a hospital in Bloomington, where Justin was airlifted to, until late last night."

"How is this friend?"

I blink away rogue tears I didn't realize I was crying. "He's going to be all right. His leg never lost circulation, something the doctor said was vital in avoiding amputation. If the machinery had fallen on his spine, he could be paralyzed or worse. All in all, it is the best possible outcome."

"How many people does this friend employ to work his land?"

"He doesn't employ anyone. It's just him and his father."

"Tell me, Marilyn, did Mr. Dunn take another position at a competing firm?"

"No, sir."

"Do you believe that working here is what Mr. Dunn truly wanted? Mr. Perkins suggested something different."

I sit taller. "Mr. Perkins is irrelevant. Working here is Rich's dream come true. The position you spoke with him about, combining farming, something that means so much to him, with wealth management was more than he could have possibly hoped for."

"And he turned down our offer...?"

"To work Justin's land. Justin is going to require physical therapy and time. He won't be able to do all that is necessary to keep his farm from being taken."

"Mr. Dunn chose to save his friend's land over taking his dream job."

Mr. Stevens didn't ask a question, but I nod. "Yes, sir. He mentioned it last night. Things were still raw, and emotions were high. We didn't know yet if Justin would recover. You see, as I mentioned, Justin is married to Rich's sister."

Mr. Stevens lets out a whistle.

"I asked Rich not to make a rash decision."

"We have called him a few times, and he hasn't answered."

I pat the bag at my side. "He left his phone in Indy when he rushed to the hospital. I am taking it to him tonight."

Mr. Stevens stands and offers me his hand. "Thank you for being up front with me. If you see Mr. Dunn..."

I smile. "I plan to."

"...please let him know we haven't yet accepted his refusal, and I'd like to speak to him when he has the time."

My smile grows. "Oh, thank you, Mr. Stevens. I didn't realize your family farmed." When he looks at me quizzically, I add, "Rich told me."

"My grandfather loved and respected the land. I didn't follow in his footsteps, and it's worked out well. However, creating an agricultural wealth management plan has been a pipe dream of mine for some time. I'm not ready to give up that dream. Do you know anyone who has the same love and respect for land and knowledge in financial planning?"

"I do."

Mr. Stevens grins. "Thank you. You better get on the road. I suspect there's more than one person waiting for you in Riverbend."

I reach for my bag and walk toward my coat. As I'm putting it on, I ask, "Have you ever been down to our small town?"

He presses his lips together. "One time. It was in the autumn. Elenore enjoys Brown County. I seem to remember a shop. Quint...something or the other. Elenore raved about the lotion she bought there for years."

"Quintessential Treasures."

"Yes," he says. "Is the store still there?"

"It is. It's owned by our friend Justin's sister."

"Small world."

"Small town," I reply.

I'm more excited to get to my hometown than I have been, possibly ever.

Chapter Twenty-Eight

Ricky
Friday morning

Having spent the night at Devan and Justin's house, I wake to the slam of the back door. Since I was the only one in the house when I went to sleep, the sound of an intruder before seven in the morning startles me and pulls me into reality. No one in Riverbend would break in to their house; then again, if word has gotten out about Justin's accident, maybe someone could think this is an opportune time to break and enter.

Living in the city has a way of making one less trusting.

The chill within the house causes goose bumps to pepper my flesh as I push back the blankets on the bed.

In my boxer briefs, I sneak down the front staircase, looking for a weapon. With each step, the wooden floor is cool under my bare feet.

Back when my parents lived here, I knew where to find a rifle. Going through Devan and Justin's closets while someone could be stealing them blind doesn't seem like a good use of my time. My heartbeat drums in my ears as I tiptoe down the staircase, hearing noises coming from Devan's new kitchen. It sounds as if someone is opening and closing cabinets.

How long until that person moves up the stairs?

Everyone knows that people are most likely to hide cash and jewelry in their bedroom.

Scanning the living room, I search for anything that could be a weapon. Hell, a baseball bat would do. My sister is either too good of a housekeeper, or married couples don't leave baseball bats and guns lying around. I search for something heavy. Finding a crystal bowl on a bookshelf, I lift it over my head. It's as I turn the corner that I come face-to-face with my mom.

She scans from the bowl down to my toes. "Richard John, what are you doing?"

"Fuck, Mom." I shake my head, lowering the crystal bowl. "Sorry. I thought someone was breaking in."

"And you were going to save the day with Devan's wedding gift?"

I look at the bowl and shrug.

Mom asks, "Would a burglar let that door slam?"

"Maybe," I say, "if they didn't think anyone was home."

"Your car is parked outside."

I set the bowl on the kitchen counter. "It's too early for logic."

Mom waves her hand up and down. "Maybe you could put on pants and a shirt before fighting criminals."

"Do you think they'd wait? Like I could call out 'Hey, I'm coming down with a dangerous weapon, but I need to get dressed first. So, could you maybe wait?'"

"It's better if you're polite. Always say please." She lifts an eyebrow. "*Please* put on more clothes."

I tilt my chin toward the coffeepot. "I'll put on clothes if you make us coffee."

"Deal."

As I turn to go back upstairs, I stop. "Any news on Justin?"

"Last I heard, Justin was in a lot of pain. They finally got the dosage of pain meds working, and he's getting some sleep this morning." Mom sighs. "Devan says she's not leaving the hospital."

I nod. "Yeah, that's what she told me."

"I'm here to get her some clothes and things."

"I was going to go visit."

"Call your sister first. Maybe you can take a bag to her."

I press my lips together and shake my head. "No phone, remember?"

"Oh, is Marilyn going to get that for you?"

Marilyn.

"I didn't ask her to. It's better if we back things off for a while."

Mom's expression saddens. "Why?"

"We can't date if I'm here and she's in Indy."

"It's hardly long-distance. It's basically an hour-and-a-half drive. There are people in Florida who commute that long to and from work each day. Of course, it's only like twenty miles, but the traffic..."

Not interested in facts about my parents' second home state, I turn back to the staircase. "I'll go put on pants. *Please*" —I use her word— "make coffee. I need a whole pot."

Walking down the hallway, I remember Marilyn staying in the bedroom near the one where I'm staying. I think about the way her lips were parted as she slept and the way she tried to contain her noises and sounds in the shower.

Fuck.

Those thoughts won't accomplish anything other

than making me need a cold shower. I rub my hands up and down my arms. "Why is it so cold?"

I throw on a pair of blue jeans, pull yesterday's thermal over my head, and slip my feet into socks. Once I'm back downstairs, I hear the coffeepot spitting and spurting. Mom is in the living room putting wood into the woodstove in the fireplace. "Shit," I say. "That's why it's so cold in here."

"You need to keep kindling going."

"Thanks, Mom. I didn't know how a woodstove works."

She shoots me a side-eye. "If you're planning on moving in to their house, you better figure it out."

"I'm not moving in. I'm taking care of it for them."

"You know, your dad and I can do that."

"You have your place in Florida."

Mom closes the glass front on the woodstove. Behind the small window in the door, sparks crackle, creating flames. She stands and dusts her hands, one against the other. "Dad and I can stay here, Ricky. Both of our houses are relatively maintenance-free. If Devan needs us, we'll be here. You have a life."

A life.

A job.

A girlfriend.

I look around to see what time it is. "Can I use your phone? I need to call someone."

"Sure," she says, walking back into the kitchen, taking her phone from her purse and handing it my direction. "Here."

"I have the number upstairs." With her phone in hand, I hurry back to the bedroom and pull out my laptop. A quick search and I have the number to call Parker and Stevens. I hit the appropriate buttons to get me to Mr. Stevens's assistant.

"...please leave a message."

I take a deep breath. "Hello, this is Richard Dunn. I'm sorry for calling so early. Please relay this message to Mr. Parker and Mr. Stevens. I am thankful that they expressed confidence in me. I'm certain their agricultural wealth plan will be beneficial for all." I pause. "Another opportunity has come up, rather unexpectedly. I regretfully must decline your offer." Before I can change my mind, I disconnect the call.

Life postponed.

Job gone.

That leaves one loose end.

I can't think about Marilyn or Justin right this minute. It's too much. I don't want to lose her, and I don't want Justin and Devan to lose their livelihood. Those thoughts and more had me tossing and turning all night. It doesn't take a wealth manager to know that

Devan's teacher's salary won't carry them through an entire year.

By the time I make it back to the kitchen, the first floor is warming nicely. I hand Mom back her phone. "Thanks."

She pours us each a cup of coffee, looking in the refrigerator for cream and handing me the cup with black coffee. "Your dad wants to stay and help Justin with the farm."

"No, you and Dad broke free."

"So did you, Rick." She sits at the kitchen table and pats the seat next to her at the head of the table.

Begrudgingly, I take the seat.

"Your dad and I are parents, first and foremost. Jack isn't a spring chicken, but he was doing what needed to be done two years ago. Justin is going to need every willing hand."

"He's got me and Randy." I think about what Marilyn said. "Dax will help when he can. Hell, I'm sure all the guys will." Meeting Mom's stare, I add, "Someone needs to take the reins. Until Justin can be that someone, I'm going to take the role."

"Have you talked to Justin about this?"

I shake my head.

"Marilyn?"

"We're not that serious, Mom."

"Oh really? Does she know that?"

I push the chair from the table. "I'm going to take a shower, and then I'll head to Bloomington. I doubt Justin is in the mood to chat, but I'll talk to him. He needs to concentrate on getting better, not worrying about what is happening here."

"Neither Justin nor Devan will want you to put your life on hold for them."

"I'm not asking. I'm telling."

It's after nine when I pull into the visitor parking lot at the hospital in Bloomington. Carrying the bag Mom packed for Devan, I check in at the front desk and make my way to Justin's room. With a deep breath, I push in the door and step into the room.

Justin's leg is lifted by chains and pullies. His eyes are closed, and Devan is curled up in a reclining chair, looking like a kitten under a blanket. Not wanting to wake anyone, I take the bag into the room and open the closet.

"Hi," Devan says softly.

"Shit," I whisper. "I didn't mean to wake you."

My sister stretches, pushing up her arms and fisting her hands.

"I'm sure you didn't get much sleep."

"Not much," Justin says. "Why are you here and not in Indy?"

"Because of you, asshole."

Devan throws the blanket to the side. “Is that bag for me?”

“Yeah,” I say, handing it her direction. “Mom put it together this morning.”

My sister takes the strap of the bag. “I’m going to go into the bathroom and try to feel human.” She lowers her voice as she steps near me. “See if you can talk to him.”

I nod and turn my attention to Justin. “How you doing?”

He shakes his head. “I’m fucked up. I fucked up.”

My lips curl. “It’s a mess, but it’s fixable.”

Justin turns his face away.

I step closer. “This could be a lot worse than a leg.”

The muscles in his face flex as he clenches his jaw.

“Talk to me.”

Justin turns back in my direction, his eyes blazing. “If I was dead, at least she’d get insurance money. This —” he motions toward his leg “—I promised to take care of her. I told you I would. Now, I’ve fucked it all up.”

“You did promise me. I expect you to keep your word.”

He lays his head back and stares up at the ceiling. “The life I never knew I wanted was right here. It’s gone.” He turns to me. “Do you know we’ve been talking about kids? What a fucking joke. I can't even support Devan and myself."

"How long are they talking?" I ask. "Until you're back on your feet?"

Justin shakes his head. "No one has said a damn thing."

"Well, here's the thing," I say, pulling a chair up beside the hospital bed. "You've never lied to me." Justin's gaze comes my way. "So I fully expect you to get better and keep your word—to me, to Devan, to your dad, and to the bank." His eyes close. "And while you're getting better, you're going to have to put up with my sorry ass."

Justin's forehead furrows. "What? Why?"

"I'm moving in with you. So, that honeymoon you and Devan had is over. I figure this is January. By late summer, you'll be back to your usual miserable self, and that's when I was supposed to graduate. I'll save money getting rid of that apartment, and I'll let you and Devan feed me."

"No fucking way."

"Did I ask?"

"Shit," Justin says, wiping his nose with the back of his hand. "What about working for that firm, the one where Marilyn works? And what about Marilyn?"

"I didn't get the job."

"You didn't? Marilyn told Devan she thought you would."

I shrug. "Nope. Divine intervention. I'm jobless, and you have a job for me to do."

Justin closes his eyes, drops his chin forward, and swallows, his Adam's apple bobbing.

I go on. "I'm going to need to understand where everything stands. You'll need to give me your passwords so I can access all your reports, your proposed P&L, and your bank accounts."

"You going to rob us?" Devan asks, coming from the bathroom. She's wearing clean clothes, and her hair is wet.

"No," Justin says. "He's moving in."

Devan's eyes widen. "What about your job?"

"I didn't get it."

Her shoulders slump. "Rick, I'm so sorry."

"Don't be. I have a new job—it's called foreman of the Sheers farm."

Seven hours later, my back and neck ache, but I've gotten myself up to speed on Justin's financials. I lean back against the office chair that used to belong to my father and scroll through more financial reports on Justin's computer. I've made notes and checked prices for seed, pre-emergent herbicide, fertilizer. Calculating the amount needed of each and multiplying that by the number of acres. I've been sitting here since a little after ten this morning.

I may not have been completely truthful with Devan and Justin, but the truth is that I wasn't hired for the position I interviewed for. Telling them I didn't get the job wasn't a complete lie.

More time passes as I get a feel for what needs to be done to keep Justin and Devan in the black and our family farm out of auction. Back in the living room, I remember to add wood to the woodstove. Outside, the sky is dark. I could go into town and get dinner at the diner or go to my parents' house, but after a day of staring at the computer screen, I'm okay with finding something to eat in their refrigerator. Hell, with the way Justin eats, there should be plenty of food.

Through the kitchen window, I see headlights coming down the lane.

Chapter Twenty-Nine

Marilyn

Driving to Riverbend via Bloomington isn't exactly a direct route, but I made it. After a stop at the hospital to see both Justin and Devan, I'm now driving up the lane to their house. Devan told me that Ricky didn't get the job at Parker and Stevens, and instead, he was going to work for Justin until Justin is well again.

Seeing the expression on Devan's face and hearing her voice as she told me what a difference Ricky's offer made to Justin, I didn't have the heart to tell her that Ricky lied. Ricky was offered a job, better than the one he interviewed for.

I pull up next to Devan's house like I've done all my life. The lights are on in the kitchen. There is something about it that fills me with contentment. Devan and Justin have changed it, but the house still holds the glow of the home it's always been.

My overnight bag is in the back seat. Biting my lip, I debate whether to take it up to the house with me. I don't want to assume that Ricky wants me to stay. Then again, it is the weekend, and last weekend, he stayed at my place.

Grabbing my purse and the overnight bag, I throw the straps over my shoulder and walk through the chill of the night up onto the back porch. Without knocking, I open the screen door and then the solid door.

"Hi," I say, seeing Ricky sitting at the kitchen table. I begin to unbutton my coat.

Ricky inhales and stands. "You didn't need to come back."

"I wanted to for Devan...and you." Setting the overnight bag on the floor, I dig into my purse. "I brought you your phone and charger. I stopped by your apartment this morning."

His hair is standing up as if he's been running his fingers through it, but it's the tiredness in his eyes and the slowness in his step that catch my attention.

I lift the phone and charger toward him and tilt my head. "Are you okay?"

He comes closer, taking the phone. "Thank you.

You didn't need to do that." The energy and vitality that differentiates Ricky are what is missing.

"I miss your text messages, and you can't text without a phone."

His forehead lowers. "Marilyn, I..." He inhales and runs his fingers through his hair before straightening his shoulders. "I'm going to move out of my apartment. I talked to Justin, and I'm going to do what I said."

I swallow. "Devan told me about your offer to Justin. She said it means a lot."

Ricky shrugs.

I take a step closer. "I brought my overnight bag. I didn't want to assume, but you stayed at my place last weekend. And it's not like we didn't already christen their shower."

"I don't think it's a good idea."

"Don't push me away, Ricky. We can make it through this."

He turns a complete circle and faces me, his tone louder. "No. I made a move on you because I thought I could actually be someone...someone you would be proud to be with."

My chest aches and my throat constricts. "You are."

"I'm going backward, Marilyn." His words grow louder. "I'm not going to pull you down with me."

I raise my voice to match his. "You're not going backward. You're helping a friend."

He lifts his arms and swings them from side to side. "I'm back in my childhood home."

"Yes, you are. You're here because you chose to be. That's not backward." When he doesn't respond, I tilt my chin toward his phone. "There are calls on there from Mr. Stevens."

"You snooped in my phone?"

"No," I say quickly. "I spoke to Mr. Stevens this afternoon."

"About what?"

I sigh, unsure why he isn't seeing the bigger picture. "About you."

"What the hell, Marilyn? You have no right."

Stepping closer, I reach out, laying my hand on his chest. "Ricky, it's not bad. It's good. Mr. Stevens came to me."

He steps back from my touch and shakes his head. "What's good about what happened? What's good about Justin in the hospital or me missing the opportunity I wanted?"

I force a smile. "That's the thing. Once I explained the situation to Mr. Stevens..."

Ricky runs his fingers over his facial hair and stares at me. "It was none of your fucking business to do that. I don't want a job because you got it for me.

Fuck, people are going to think I slept my way into the position."

My blood heats at his insanity. "Really? Did you fuck Mr. Stevens? Or was it Mr. Parker?"

"No. You know what I mean!" he yells, louder than necessary.

"Of course you didn't." My flesh feels tight at this unexpected argument. "You showed them that you have a subset of knowledge they've been looking for."

Ricky shakes his head. "Unbelievable."

"I didn't get you the job. *You* got you the job. I just gave Mr. Stevens the information to understand why you would turn down such a great offer."

Ricky clenches his jaw. "You want me to take the job and leave Justin to lose everything?"

I stare in disbelief. "Do you think I want Justin and Devan to lose everything?" I motion around the newly renovated kitchen. "Look what they've done. I want them to keep the farm and for you to have the position you want."

His lips come together as the muscles pull tight in his jaw. "I see. You want me to have that position, because you don't want to tell people you're dating a farmer."

"What the hell?"

"That's it. You've wanted out of Riverbend for as long as I can remember. The last thing you want is for me to be back here. So you went out of your way to smooth things over behind my back and get me a job that you find more prestigious."

Turning around, I lift my overnight bag strap to my shoulder. "Fuck you, Ricky Dunn. I don't know if you're full of yourself or you're drowning in disappointment. Mr. Stevens came to me. I answered his questions. If you weren't so damn deep in your pity party, you might realize that what I did was for you, not for me. You really think my friends would give a shit if I dated a farmer? Maybe you've forgotten, but one of my best friends is married to a farmer."

"Marilyn." His tone is softer.

"Go to hell." I fight the tears pricking the backs of my eyes. "I gave you another chance. I only asked for one thing—not to hurt me again. Well, congratulations, you're hurting me by pushing me away. Have a nice fucking life." Spinning toward the door, I open the solid door and push open the screen.

The door slams behind me.

I'm not sure if Ricky follows me or not. I don't turn around or even look at the house until I'm in my car. My hands tremble on the steering wheel. Despite my blurry vision, I throw the car into reverse and do a three-point turn. My foot slams down on the gas pedal, leaving Ricky behind, where I should have kept him.

At the end of the lane by the white barn, I stop the car and send my mom a text message.

Sorry for the short notice. I visited the hospital, but I need to get back to Carmel. The new tax rules were just released. I have a weekend of exciting reading.

I even add a laughing emoji.

Hitting my playlist, I listen to that new album again. The tears keep me from singing, but I don't need to. I can feel the words "My Boy Only Breaks His Favorite Toys" in my soul.

My body is still shaking by the time I make it back to my apartment. I'm not even sure how I made it home. The entire drive is a blur. Grabbing my bags, I walk back into my apartment building and, finally, into my apartment.

After locking the door, I allow myself the breakdown I was trying to temper in the car. With my back against the door, I slide to the floor. My overnight bag and purse are at my side as I pull my knees to my chest and lower my forehead.

"The hell with him," I tell myself.

Reaching for my phone, I want to call someone who will understand. I realize I can't call Devan. She has enough to worry about, and in the depths of my soul, I don't want to call Jill and admit I was wrong about Ricky, that he played me again. More tears come as memories of the last few weeks replay in my mind.

"Stupid."

I was an idiot to trust him, to put my faith in him.

Digging my phone from my purse, I hold out hope that maybe he called or messaged. I don't know if I'd return his call, but...

The only message on my phone is from my mom, telling me to drive safely and let her know when I arrive. Yes, I'm a twenty-five-year-old woman who still texts her mother. I send the text message.

Home safe, Mom. Good night.

Turning off my phone, I go on a search for ice cream or wine, something to eat or drink with my bath.

Chapter Thirty

Ricky

A life.

A job.

A girlfriend.

As I stare at the bedroom ceiling through the dark, I go through that list. Life—postponed. Job—gone. Girlfriend—gone. Rolling for the hundredth time, I punch the pillow into submission and groan.

It isn't that Marilyn and I had been a couple for long, but from the first dinner, we had a familiarity that made things seem comfortable. In a Venn diagram, our overlapping knowledge and backgrounds left little to be new. Over the years, I'd grown used to her smart and sassy comments. In the last few weeks, I came to recognize her wit and the depth of her devotion.

A look at the clock tells me it's only three in the morning. Nevertheless, I don't foresee sleep in my future. Last night, after Marilyn left, I yearned to call Justin. I don't know what I wanted him to say, whether it was to say he understood why I pushed her away, or maybe I wanted to hear someone confirm that I treated her wrong and I needed to make it right.

Justin wasn't and isn't an option.

I say a prayer of thanks to the higher being that he *is* an option. Mom and I talked about what could have happened if the baler had fallen on his spine. While he is alive, the last thing he needs is to hear about my love life, or the lack thereof.

The idea of going to the diner in another few hours sparks my interest. It will be nice to see the gang of men. Today's Saturday during the winter. The table should be full.

What do I say if someone mentions Marilyn?

Do I admit I did what I never wanted to do—that I hurt her again?

Again would insinuate a first time, and they don't need to know about that.

The possibility of breakfast with the guys loses its luster.

Turning on the light next to the bed, I reach for my phone.

Marilyn said I had messages from the partners, but I haven't had the stomach to listen to them. No time like the present.

Sitting with my back against the headboard, I pull up my voice mails.

There are three from Parker and Stevens. I click on the first and listen.

"Mr. Dunn, this is Tillie Johnson, Mr. Ralph Stevens's assistant. We received your message. The partners are disappointed and wish you well in the future."

Nice. Concise. To the point.

In other words, "Don't let the door hit you in the ass."

The next message was left two hours after the first.

"Richard, Herold Parker here. We understand you have found something other than Parker and Stevens. If you'd be willing to discuss your decision, we may be able to counter-offer."

I sit taller. That is unexpected.

"Fuck," I mumble.

The third message was received at five twenty last night.

"Richard, this is Ralph Stevens. Please call my office Monday morning. Herold and I have spoken about your situation. We'd like to discuss options with you."

I shake my head.

It about killed me to make the call yesterday morning and decline their offer. I'm not sure I have it in me to do it again. Beyond the panes of glass, the wind blows. Closing my eyes, I listen to the creaks of the old house. In this house is where I lived most of my life. There's undeniable comfort within the walls that isn't duplicatable beyond.

Yet, living in Indianapolis filled me with different emotions.

I'll even admit, if only to myself, that fear was one of the feelings. Fear of the unknown. Leaving Riverbend was like leaving a bubble of security. The guys meeting for breakfast later this morning are part of that bubble.

A cushion.

Protection.

While leaving that familiar safety net elicited fear, it also provoked excitement.

Being an older student wasn't easy. Hell, some of my professors were younger than me. However, I never expected easy. As one of my professors said, I possessed a determination to succeed beyond that of most of the younger students. Not only did I and do I want to learn, but I'm also enthusiastic to learn.

I think about things Marilyn said…I had a career before entering the world of finance. That experience is what Ralph Stevens and Herold Parker saw. Sheepishly, I make the decision to give them a call on Monday morning.

By seven thirty, I'm jacked up on too much coffee as I enter the diner on Main Street.

"Ricky," Joyce, the owner and best waitress, says from behind the counter.

I see a few familiar faces at the counter and filling the booths. The round table near the back is empty, but it's set up for the normal crowd. As I walk toward Joyce, I get a few waves. Everyone else goes back to their breakfast.

"I heard a rumor you were in town." Her smile dims. "How is Justin doing?"

"I haven't spoken to him today. Yesterday…" I'm about to say he was feeling sorry for himself, but I can't make the words form. Marilyn said I was doing the same. She may have been right, and fuck, I didn't have a ten-ton piece of machinery fall on me. "Yesterday, he was still hurting."

Joyce shakes her head. "It's a miracle."

I take a seat at the counter. "Seems like a tragedy, if you ask me."

"Don't you remember Alvin Gordon?"

My lips come together. "Bruce Gordon's brother?" I'd forgotten about him. "Way before my time."

"Mine too," she says with a smile, setting a cup in front of me and pouring coffee. "Goodness, it was probably sixty years ago now. He was younger than Justin. Something malfunctioned in the silo. The poor man drowned in corn..."

I grimace, thinking of a scene from a movie. "You're right, Joyce. Justin will recover. That's a miracle."

The bell above the door jingles.

"Ricky," Cory Sims calls, coming closer and patting me on the shoulder. "We were hoping you'd show this morning."

I nod to Joyce and take my cup, following Cory to the back table. "Who are *we*?"

Cory's eyes circle the table. "About everyone. Dax has been organizing people to help at the Sheers farm."

"He has?"

"You know Dax. He has spreadsheets and shit." Cory laughs.

"Fuck," I mumble. "I suppose I should have reached out to Dax."

The bell above the door jingles as Dax Richards and Nick Dancy walk in together. Looking up, I think about how different the two men are. Dax is an attorney and does some shit with a title company. Nick is a plumber. On a cold Saturday morning, they are just two friends. A few steps behind, Mick Reynolds and Harvey Russel enter.

"Ricky," Dax says, taking a chair across the table. "I'm glad you're here."

"Cory tells me that you and I need to talk."

"About Justin and the farm?" Dax asks.

I nod. "I'm taking a sabbatical. I'll be here until harvest or when Justin is ready to take over."

Dax leans across the table. "I heard you were hired by Parker and Stevens in north Indy. That's an accomplishment. You shouldn't waste it."

My lie about not getting the job is on the tip of my tongue.

Nick saves me by jumping in. "You know, Rick. You and Dax will make a good team, and we're all willing to do what we can. Maybe then you can put off that sabbatical."

I lift my coffee cup toward Dax. "Let's talk." Justin married my sister, and Dax married Justin's sister. That's Riverbend. "Family."

"Family." Dax smiles and lifts his cup.

I didn't believe I was feeling sorry for myself, but the shock and relief of knowing I won't be doing this alone alleviates stress I didn't realize I was carrying. It is probably similar to the relief Justin felt when we spoke yesterday. Maybe there's a way to save my job in the process.

If there is, I know who I owe for that possibility.

Regret is a bitter pill early in the morning, especially mixed with coffee.

"What do you boys want to eat?" Joyce asks, walking around the table and taking orders.

Cory elbows me after I give Joyce my order. "Are the rumors true about you and Marilyn James?"

Probably not anymore.

Chapter Thirty-One

Marilyn
A week later

"Have you been home?" I ask Devan, seated across the table from her in the hospital cafeteria.

She nods. "Once or twice. It's nice knowing Ricky is there and the house isn't empty."

Devan pushes the leaves of her salad around in the bottom of the plastic container. When she looks up through veiled lashes, I know what's coming.

"What happened between you two?"

Ricky and I aren't a subject I've spoken to anyone about. Not even Jill. Everyone is too close to the epicenter of our tale. I'm also scared that if I start to talk about it, the waterworks will begin again. It took two days and so many hot baths that I was pruney before I could wear eye makeup.

"We decided that it wasn't a good idea." I shrug. "Nothing more and nothing less."

Devan shakes her head. "I love you, Marilyn, but I don't believe you."

I swallow the lump forming in my throat. "You don't need to worry about it. Your plate is a little full. Tell me how Justin is doing."

Devan goes on to talk about his ups and downs. There were concerns about blood clots, and the medicine they had him on didn't agree with his blood pressure. Despite his leg being immobilized, they've begun physical therapy. After he is released from the hospital, he is supposed to go to a rehab facility.

"Of course," she says, "he doesn't want to do that. He wants to be out on the farm. He said if he can't do the physical labor, at least he can do the business side."

"I'm sure it's in good hands with Ricky." I inwardly cringe as I say his name.

"Didn't I tell you? It isn't just Ricky. He and Dax have been working together, and..." She shakes her head. "They have been a godsend. Dax has arranged to move his clients around. Unless he has a closing at his title company, he is spending two full days a week devoted to the farm. Dad and Randy Sheers are pitching in wherever they can. And that will let Ricky spend three days a week in Indy."

My heart aches.

"I didn't know he was going to do that."

Devan's eyes grow wide. "He said he didn't get the job, but something happened last week. I don't understand it all…you probably would. From what Rick said, Parker and Stevens is interested in creating a new something or other…"

I nod, knowing what she means. It's an agricultural wealth perspective proposal.

"And since it is new," Devan goes on, "they agreed to lengthen the timeline and allow Rick to work part time while still spending time here."

Swallowing, I feign a smile. "It sounds like things are working out."

"Justin's friends are pledging their time and energy. I know it makes Justin uncomfortable. We talked about it. If the positions were reversed, Justin said he'd do all he could to help. I told him to suck it up and accept the help of others." She looks down at her salad and back up. "I'm going back to school next week. I hate to leave Justin, but I'm not a lot of help, and I think space would be good."

My eyebrow shoots up. "Are you two okay?"

Devan nods fast. "We will be. It's not easy with him injured and me feeling sick."

"Are you sick? Maybe it's just the stress."

"I thought the same thing. When I told Mom to pack a few things, I asked her to pack tampons and other things I thought I'd need."

"Oh shit." I cover my lips with my fingertips. "You're pregnant."

She presses her lips together and nods. Suddenly, her eyes are glossy.

I jump from my chair, hurry to her side of the table, and wrap her in a hug. "I love you."

"Love you too," she says, her words muffled against my shoulder.

Pushing her shoulders back, I look her in the eye. "This is good, right? I mean, I know Jill never wants children, but you..."

"It's good. The timing is terrible. I tried to keep it from Justin—just for a little while—but it's hard to hide that I'm puking up my breakfast before I've even eaten it. I swear, the nausea started before I was even late."

"You've taken a test?"

"I have. The nurses got one for me. I guess there's nothing more official than a hospital pregnancy test." She blinks away her tears. "I wish Justin were more excited. He was the one talking about children."

"Wow," I say, concentrating on my friend. "You

two know how to keep things exciting. Have you told Jill?"

"Not yet. Please don't say anything. Other than Justin and my parents, no one knows. I'm still very early...you understand?"

"Of course," I say, concentrating on the most positive news in a long time. "I know if it's a girl, you'll want to name her after me. But I need to warn you, Marilyn is an old name, and you know those cute license plates kids get for bicycles?" I shake my head. "She won't be able to have one. If she does, it will have stick-on letters, and that isn't the same."

"Thanks for the warning," Devan says. She pushes away the salad container. "Believe me, extra hormones aren't what I need right now."

Moving back to my chair, I reach out and cover her hand with mine. "What you need is to know everything will be all right. And it sounds like Ricky and Dax have the farm covered. Justin will improve as he is able to move around more, and as for you, my friend, you need to take care of yourself."

"It will be good to go home more. I hate being there without Justin."

"He'll be home soon." I look down at what's left of our lunches. "Will he mind if I visit him? I need to go back home. The joys of tax season are all around."

"My least favorite holiday," Devan says.

"Mine too. I'm spending hours reading about ways to save my clients money."

"Don't you have to be rich to have a wealth manager?"

"That's subjective."

"I know, but shouldn't people who don't make as much money be able to find the loopholes?"

"You're being too rational," I say as we carry our trays to the conveyor belt.

A few minutes later, Devan pushes the door to Justin's room open and stops in her tracks. "Ricky, I didn't realize you would be here."

I suck in a breath, seeing him over Devan's shoulder. His brown eyes are on me for longer than I want. My heart is beating in double time as I push past my friend and turn to Justin. "Hey, I wanted to say hi, before I head back north."

Justin looks between me and Ricky in a way that tells me Ricky's been as forthcoming with his friends as I have.

Ricky clears his throat. "I was going to leave. You can stay."

Pressing my lips together and keeping my vision on Justin, I say, "Don't go out of your way for me, and I won't go out of my way for you."

"Marilyn…" Ricky's tone makes me want to turn, but I don't.

"How are you feeling?" I ask Justin, doing my best to ignore the other man in the room.

"Confused," Justin replies. "What the hell is happening?"

"Absolutely nothing," I say before anyone else can answer. I walk forward and squeeze Justin's hand. "Get better soon." I want to say something about the baby, but from what Devan said, Ricky doesn't know. I'm not going to be the one to spill the beans. "I need to head home. I'll see you later."

"Thanks, Marilyn," Justin says.

I spin as I hear my name again from Ricky, but I don't stop until I'm at the elevators. Devan is close on my heels.

"Talk to me," she says.

I know I can't talk, not to Devan or anyone. If I so much as open my lips, I'll cry again. Instead, I shake my head and push the button again. The doors open, and I hurry in, turning to wave goodbye to my friend.

Chapter Thirty-Two

Ricky
Two weeks later

My office doesn't have a window, not even one the size of a porthole. Nevertheless, it is a room with a door, not a cubicle. With my suit coat hanging on the back of my chair, I stare at the information on my desk, completely in awe that I am sitting where I am. This is almost everything I want in life.

The missing piece is no doubt on the third floor. I can't blame her for not speaking to me two weeks ago in Justin's hospital room. I haven't tried to call or text her. That doesn't mean I haven't written at least a hundred different messages, only to delete each one. I said things to Marilyn that no one deserves to hear. If I were into therapy, I might learn my reasons for pushing her away.

It doesn't take a psychology degree to know that I was freaked out about putting my career on hold while simultaneously worried about the future of my sister, my best friend, and my family farm. Marilyn told me not to make any rash decisions.

I've lain awake at night, thinking about how she was right. If only I'd taken the time to talk to Dax, Dad, and Randy Sheers. For some reason, in my mind, I was the only one who could save the Sheers farm. I was so focused on the fucking trees, I didn't see the forest.

Maybe my desire to move beyond Riverbend wouldn't allow me to see the positives it has to offer, friendships and family.

Being able to both help Justin and begin my career seemed like an unachievable dream. I lean back against the desk chair and look at the small office. I have a bookshelf and one other chair facing my desk. There is one plant on the corner of my desk from Mom. She always was into plants.

In a nutshell, it's the best fucking office in the world.

A knock on the door pulls me back to the present. "Come in."

I sit taller as Bryce Perkins enters. "Dunn, I have some forms I need you to complete."

Reaching for the stack of papers, I say, "It was nice of you to personally deliver these."

"As the co-chair of the talent acquisition team, I thought it was best that the two of us have a few words."

I gesture to my other chair. "Have a seat."

Bryce lifts his chin, turning a circle and scanning the entirety of my office. "It's nice they could clean out this broom closet for you."

"More than nice. It's perfect." I look down at the forms. They seem pretty straightforward. "What would you like to discuss? I'm busy acclimating myself with the files from Mr. Stevens."

Bryce is still standing. "Leave Marilyn alone."

The hairs on the back of my neck stand to attention. "Excuse me?"

"You heard me."

I stand on my side of the desk. "Is controlling Marilyn in the job description of co-chair of the talent acquisition team?"

"This isn't about control. I told her what we all saw at the dinner. You used her. I warned her. She didn't listen. At least she listened when I told her that after you break her heart, I'll be the one to put it back together."

With each of his words and phrases, I clench my jaw tighter. "Keep dreaming. I know for a fact Marilyn isn't interested in you."

"We have a date next week on Valentine's Day. I'd say your information is outdated." Before I can respond, he says, "Just stay away from her. If you don't, I'll tell the partners that I've received complaints about you being inappropriate with senior female employees."

"Are you threatening me?"

He smiles. "I like to think of it as a friendly reminder." He turns away. "Oh, and have those forms to Jen, my assistant, by four this afternoon." He leaves the door open in his wake.

"Fucker."

Valentine's Day.

Shit, I've been too busy to even know what month it is, much less a holiday. Throughout the day, my attention deviates from the project before me to thoughts of Marilyn.

I try to tell myself that Bryce is better for her. He has a better job. He's been here longer. It doesn't matter how many stupid reasons I come up with; I can't shake the feeling that he's not the best man for Marilyn. He can't be.

I am.

The question is if it's too late.

Near the end of the workday, I find myself on the elevator, pushing the number three. Stepping onto the third floor, I approach the receptionist's desk and flash a smile at Klara. "Hello, Klara. Is Ms. James in?"

Klara smiles as if she remembers me. "It's been a while." She points at me. "Letter guy."

"Guilty," I say, lifting my hands.

"Let me check to see if she's busy."

Nodding, I step back. As Klara touches buttons on her headset, the door to the back hallway opens and Marilyn emerges. For a moment, I'm starstruck, knowing I am an idiot to have pushed her out of my life. From her deep brown hair, her striking eyes and gorgeous smile, down her sensual curves and her shapely legs, I want her.

Before I can step forward or even speak, Bryce comes out of the door, laying his hand in the small of her back.

"Ms. James," Klara calls.

Marilyn steps away from Bryce's touch.

I can't stand to see any more as I turn away and hit the button for the elevator. Facing the silver front, I stand stone-still until the door opens. I quickly step inside, only turning to see Marilyn's frown as the doors close.

An idea comes to me. The problem is that I will never be able to get Marilyn to my apartment. I kept it, with my three days a week in Carmel. By the time I make it to my apartment, my mind is made up.

Just like I didn't need to save Justin by myself, for my plan to work, I'm going to need help. Today is Wednesday, but Friday night will have to do. I hit the contact and call my sister. She answers on the first ring.

"Devan, I need your help."

Chapter Thirty-Three

Marilyn

My mind is coming up with too many horrible scenarios. The message I received from Devan said that Justin had been moved to a rehabilitation center in Washington, Indiana. Her mom had flown back to Florida, and she needed me at her house as soon as I could be there. After work, I swung by home and packed an overnight bag. The traffic on the north side of Indianapolis was horrendous. It seemed like every driver was trying to get out of the city. Intrastate, interstate, highway, or street, it didn't matter.

Now, I'm only about fifteen minutes away from her house, but I haven't been able to reach her by phone or text message. I'm more than a little scared that something is the matter with her or the baby.

My focus on Devan has kept my other constant thought from my mind, if only temporarily. That thought would be about Ricky.

It would be a lie to say I didn't check on his position at Parker and Stevens. It made my heart happy and sad that he'd worked out a compromise with the partners. From Devan, I also learned that Ricky wasn't the only one shouldering the responsibilities of the farm. Ricky Dunn may be an ass, but in my opinion, he deserves to be happy. I remember the way he looked, his eyes shone, and his dimples grew when he spoke about the possibilities for the agricultural wealth proposal.

Researching and developing the proposition is exactly something he is meant to do.

Then we're back to the fact that he's an ass.

I meant to ask Devan if Ricky would be down here. Actually, I did ask. She hasn't returned any of my messages since I said I'd hurry to Riverbend. Leaving the street, I turn down the lane toward Justin's and her house, passing by the big white barn. Nothing much has changed because it's still winter. That doesn't mean Dax and Ricky haven't been working. I'm aware there are always projects year-round.

My headlights cut through the darkness. I hold my

breath as I search the driveway for cars. At the sight of Devan's car, and only her car, I exhale. Lights are illuminating the kitchen as I hurriedly park and rush toward the house. Opening the screen door and then the solid one, I call out her name.

The house is quiet and filled with a delicious aroma of something garlic.

"Devan," I call up the back stairs. A quick search of the first floor, and I dash up the front staircase toward her bedroom. In my mind's eye, I see her alone and hurt. It's almost too much after what happened to Justin. "Devan," I call again.

At the top of the stairs, I come to a screeching halt at the sight of the man in the hallway.

"Marilyn," Ricky says, his deep voice causing the tiny hairs on my arms to stand to attention, small lightning rods sparked by the electricity in the air.

"Where's Devan?"

With the light from the end of the hall around him, Ricky seems larger-than-life, filling the width of the upstairs hallway. He's not dressed in the work clothes I saw him in the other day. Now he's wearing his low-riding blue jeans and a caramel-colored thermal that pulls tight across his wide chest and shoulders.

"Where is Devan?" I repeat louder.

"I don't know. I think she's in Washington with Justin."

"Is she okay?" Before he can answer, I ask, "Is the baby okay?"

Ricky's forehead furrows. "Baby?"

"She left me a message saying I needed to hurry down here. I'm afraid there's something wrong with the baby or her."

He comes closer and reaches for my shoulders. "I don't know about a baby, but Devan is fine."

I try to break away. "Shit. Don't tell her I told. I need to find her."

He doesn't release me. "Marilyn, she lured you down here for me."

"Why?"

"Because I was afraid if I asked, you wouldn't come."

I roll my eyes. "Oh my God. You're right, Ricky." I spin and head toward the front steps.

"Wait," he calls, his footsteps seconds behind mine. At the bottom of the stairs, he again reaches for me, this time capturing my hands. He tilts his head, his brown eyes bigger than normal. "Please, hear me out."

Taking a step back, I cross my arms over my breasts. "Make it fast."

"Do you have a date?"

My eyes narrow. "First, none of your business."

"Bryce Perkins came to me."

I exhale and shake my head. "Bryce is a douchebag."

"You're not dating him again?"

I wrinkle my nose. "No." I look around, taking in the first floor more than I did when I rushed in. A dozen roses are in a vase on the kitchen counter. The light is on in the dining room. I peer around the corner and see the table set for two with candles. "Is this all because of Bryce?"

"No." He runs his hands over his facial hair. "Yes."

Shaking my head, I make my way toward the back door.

"Marilyn, I'm an ass."

"Nice, Ricky. We can agree on something."

"I wanted the position at Parker and Stevens, not just to work there, but to be closer to you. I told you the truth when I confessed that, years ago, I didn't think I was good enough for you. I thought, maybe if we worked together…"

"It's too late."

He inhales, his nostrils flaring. "I know it should be. No matter where I work or what I do, I don't deserve you, but I want you."

Closing my eyes, I inhale, taking in the garlic aroma. "I won't let you hurt me again."

"I don't want to hurt you. I want to have a life with you, the rest of our lives." He lifts his hand.

"Don't freak out. That's not a proposal. It's me hoping that one day you may listen to one of those."

"Why?"

"Why do I want you to listen?"

"No." I shake my head. "Why would you want to say one?"

"Because I want to be with you. You make me smile. I make you smile."

"YouTube videos make me smile too."

He cocks his head to the side and grins a radiant smile. "I made chicken fettuccine alfredo. We have breadsticks, and in the freezer is a half gallon of caramel ice cream. Just caramel. I called Kandace. She's added specialty foods to Quintessential Treasures. She said Ruth had a recipe. Joyce agreed to make it."

"Homemade caramel ice cream? Why would you go to that trouble?"

"Because," he says, slowly reaching for my hand, "one night a while ago, I had a dinner with a beautiful woman. I asked her to describe her perfect date. I thought she'd describe a fabulous night in Paris or New York. Instead, she described a homemade dinner with carbs and caramel ice cream."

Tears prick my eyes. "You remembered that?"

"I'm sorry, Marilyn. I'm sorry I pushed you away. I don't have an excuse. When Justin was hurt, I thought it was all on me to make things right. That baler was ours, and it's always had trouble with the suspension. I thought we'd told him, but if we hadn't and that was why he was hurt, it was up to me and me alone to make things right."

I shake my head. "It was an accident, Ricky. It wasn't your fault."

"I know that. I've spent many hours out in the barn. The suspension isn't why it fell. It was—" he shakes his head "—an accident. The jack gave way. Who knows if it wasn't set properly or if it malfunctioned. And it took me opening my eyes to realize that helping Justin wasn't my job alone. So many people have volunteered, and Dax is as invested as I am—family."

I swallow. "I'm happy you figured that out."

"If I'd listened to you..."

I shrug. "Some people are denser than others."

"That's not all. You told me not to make a rash decision. I did. I turned down the position at Parker and Stevens. If it weren't for you..."

"No, Ricky. They want you. See? All is well."

He takes a step closer, his cologne mingling with the garlic in a spicy scent. "Marilyn, you spoke to Mr. Stevens. He said he cornered you and it was wrong, but he didn't know what else to do. I wasn't answering my phone."

"He didn't corner me. He asked me to his office

and asked politely. He did say that I didn't need to answer."

Ricky puts his hands on my waist. When I don't back away, he pulls us closer together until I need to crane my neck to maintain eye contact. "I'll never deserve you, Marilyn, but I'd like to spend our lives trying."

My resolve is fading fast. I'm still scared. "Can I call you out when you're being an ass?"

His smile lifts his cheeks. "Every time."

"Did you really make the fettuccine?"

"I mean, I bought the noodles and the sauce, but I warmed them up."

My smile returns.

"I've missed you." His lips collide with mine as one of his hands goes to the back of my neck. I lift my hands to his strong shoulders. Our tongues mingle as my lips bruise.

When we pull apart, I say, "I've missed you too."

"Did you bring an overnight bag?" he asks, his eyebrows dancing.

"Maybe." I smirk. "Feed me first."

Chapter Thirty-Four

Ricky

I wait with bated breath as Marilyn lifts a spoon of the homemade caramel ice cream to her lips. The room is perfectly still as she closes her beautiful blue eyes. When they open, her smile grows.

"Delicious."

"Does that mean we can bring your overnight bag inside?"

"I suppose. After all, I'll need my pajamas."

"No, you won't."

She stands and wraps her arms around my torso. "Don't make me regret giving in to you."

"I promise." Inhaling, I feel the need to confess. "Years ago, I didn't know I was hurting you. We agreed to no strings."

Marilyn nods.

"This time, I knew. I thought you'd be better without me."

"Isn't that my decision?"

"That's what Mom said. Kyla gave me advice too." Marilyn's eyes open wide. "Kyla." I explain, "Remember, Max's sister? She's a psychotherapist. She also told me to communicate."

"She's the one who said you had it bad for me."

I nod.

"Then tell me that—communicate, Ricky."

Smiling, I tilt my head. "Not all communication is verbal."

"Then show me."

Taking Marilyn's hand, I lead her up the front stairs, to the room I've again claimed as my own. Neither one of us hesitates as our clothes find their way to the floor. Once we're both naked, I lift Marilyn, palming her ass as she wraps her legs around my torso. In a few steps, I have her pinned between me and the wall.

"You're beautiful."

She runs her fingers through my hair. "You make me feel that way." Her touch skirts over my shoulders. "I love your hard muscles."

Bowing my head, I suck one of her nipples, causing her to squeal. She shimmies in my grasp. When

I look up into her blue gaze, I say, "I love your soft curves."

Another dip of my head and I lose myself in the flesh of her round tits. While my fingers delve between her folds. Marilyn's whimpers fill my ears as her body bounces to my rhythm.

The bedroom echoes with noises from generations past.

There's no way to know the sounds these walls have heard. However, in this moment, I can't imagine any sound as sweet as Marilyn falling apart in my arms.

I carry her to the bed and lay her down. Her dark hair fans over the pillow as her blue stare focuses on only me. Starting at her ankles, I kiss my way up the insides of her calves and thighs. Her sweet essence glistens from her perfect pink pussy. One lap of my tongue sends shock waves through her body while directing all of my circulation to the hardening of my cock.

Climbing higher over her, I admire how truly stunning this woman is.

I should have seen her like this before.

Instead of mourning my stupidity, I marvel at the way things have come together. Speaking of coming together, I line up my cock, little by little pressing into her. Marilyn's neck arches as she accommodates my length and girth. When I'm fully buried, I bring our noses together.

Marilyn opens her eyes.

"There are a few things I should tell you."

"Now?"

A laugh bubbles from my throat. "Now."

"Okay, hurry, because you have some work to do with that massive cock."

I tip my forehead to hers. "These last few weeks, I realized something."

"Are we hurrying this conversation?"

"Listen, woman, I'm trying to tell you that I love you."

Marilyn blinks. "Don't say what you don't mean."

"I mean it. I love you."

"I love you too. And there's something I want."

"My cock?" I ask.

"Yes, but I also want strings."

Epilogue~

Marilyn
Eight months later

Ricky and I stand as Justin comes in our direction. As we were what seems like years ago, we're in the hospital waiting room. It's not just the two of us. We're surrounded by Devan and Justin's family and friends. It's a regular reunion, and unlike when we were here for Justin's accident, this is a joyous occasion.

With each step, Justin shifts his weight to the cane. A few months ago, a therapist told Justin he might never walk again. Justin proved him wrong on many counts. If his determination—or stubbornness—is anything, soon the cane will be gone too. As it is, he's driving tractors, walking fence lines, and caring for his wife. Oh, and he's constantly complaining about not playing softball.

"Tell us," Kandace says.

I reach for Ricky's hand.

"We have a boy," Justin announces. His smile is ear to ear.

Ricky and I wait as the grandparents give him hugs, and then Kandace and Dax. Finally, we step forward. Ricky lets go of my hand to embrace Justin.

I can't stop my tears.

The two men in front of me have traveled a long road together. From childhood through achieving their life's dreams. Through thick and thin, good and bad, they have been at each other's side. Today, instead of sadness, we're all filled with joy.

"What's his name?" Bridget asks.

"We haven't completely decided," Justin says.

"Come on," Ricky jokes, "you've had nine months."

"We'll announce soon." He waves to the grandparents. "They said the four of you can come back."

"Justin," Kandace says with her hand on her hip.

"You're next." He turns toward us. "And you two, too."

I watch as Bridget Sheers and Janet Dunn smile gleefully at each other, and they all follow Justin through the wide double doors.

Beyond the windows of the waiting room, the leaves on the trees are beginning to change, from green to orange, red, and yellow. In Carmel, Ricky is now living with me. The agricultural wealth perspective is a working entity. That means his days at Parker and Stevens have increased.

His work in Riverbend is nearly complete. There are still fields to harvest. Thanks to the work of many people and a good year of sunshine and rain, the Sheers farm will have a profitable harvest.

Ricky and I take our seats on the far side of the waiting room. He covers my hand with his. "You know, I was waiting until their little guy was born. I didn't want to tempt fate."

"Tempt fate?"

"Too many good things at once."

I let out a sigh. "I think we had enough difficult to warrant more good."

Ricky sits up and smiles at me. "I have something for you."

"For me?" I ask gleefully. "What?"

He removes something from his pocket. Whatever he has is hidden in his grasp. "Close your eyes and give me your hand."

"You're asking a lot."

"You can trust me."

It's taken three tries, but he's right. I trust him.

Closing my eyes, I open my hand.

Ricky takes my fingers and closes them to a fist. "Open your eyes."

"I don't feel anything..." I open my fingers. "What?"

He reaches forward and lifts the string that seems to come from somewhere. "It's a string."

"A string?"

"Pull it."

"That sounds like a bad dad joke."

His dimples show. "Trust me."

I begin to pull the string and pull and pull. I gasp as a diamond ring attached to the string falls from his pocket. "Ricky?"

He falls to his knees on the floor and, lifting the ring, asks, "Marilyn, will you spend the rest of your life with me and do me the honor of being my wife?"

Before I answer, I look around, seeing members of our family and friends watching. "You planned this?"

"As much as you can plan around the birth of a baby." He lifts his eyebrows. "Will you?"

"Yes, I will."

AND THEY LIVED...HAPPILY EVER AFTER

Thank you for reading ONE STRING, Ricky and Marilyn's story. Riverbend is full of fun stories. If you haven't read Dax and Kandace's second-chance romance, get QUINTESSENTIALLY THE ONE. Or if you haven't read how Justin and Devan came to be, get their age-gap small-town romance, ONE KISS.

Aleatha's lighter ones include many stand-alone stories. PLUS ONE, ONE NIGHT, ANOTHER ONE, MY ALWAYS ONE. Enjoy them all!

What to do now

LEND IT: Did you enjoy ONE STRING? Do you have a friend who'd enjoy ONE STRING? ONE STRING may be lent one time. Sharing is caring!

RECOMMEND IT: Do you have multiple friends who'd enjoy ONE STRING? Tell them about it! Call, text, post, tweet...your recommendation is the nicest gift you can give to an author!

REVIEW IT: Tell the world. Please go to the retailer where you purchased this book, as well as Goodreads, and write a review. Please share your thoughts about ONE STRING on:

*Amazon, ONE STRING, Customer Reviews

*Barnes & Noble, ONE STRING, Customer Reviews

*iBooks, ONE STRING, Customer Reviews

*Goodreads.com/Aleatha Romig

If you liked this book you can find more of Aleatha's Lighter Ones here: www.aleatharomig.com/aleatha-s-lighter-ones

BRUTAL VOWS:

NOW AND FOREVER

TILL DEATH DO US PART

BOUND BY A PROMISE

READY TO BINGE

SINCLAIR DUET:

REMEMBERING PASSION

September 2023

REKINDLING DESIRE

October 2023

ROYAL REFLECTIONS SERIES:

RUTHLESS REIGN

November 2022

RESILIENT REIGN

January 2023

RAVISHING REIGN

April 2023

RELEVANT REIGN

June 2023

SIN SERIES:

RED SIN

October 2021

GREEN ENVY

January 2022

GOLD LUST

April 2022

BLACK KNIGHT

June 2022

STAND-ALONE ROMANTIC SUSPENSE:

SILVER LINING

October 2022

KINGDOM COME

November 2021

DEVIL'S SERIES (Duet):

DEVIL'S DEAL

May 2021

ANGEL'S PROMISE

June 2021

WEB OF SIN:

SECRETS

October 2018

LIES

December 2018

PROMISES

January 2019

TANGLED WEB:

TWISTED

May 2019

OBSESSED

July 2019

BOUND

August 2019

WEB OF DESIRE:

SPARK

Jan. 14, 2020

FLAME

February 25, 2020

ASHES

April 7, 2020

DANGEROUS WEB:

Prequel: "Danger's First Kiss"

DUSK

November 2020

DARK

January 2021

DAWN

February 2021

* * *

THE INFIDELITY SERIES:

BETRAYAL

Book #1

October 2015

CUNNING

Book #2

January 2016

DECEPTION

Book #3

May 2016

ENTRAPMENT

Book #4

September 2016

FIDELITY

Book #5

January 2017

* * *

THE CONSEQUENCES SERIES:

CONSEQUENCES

(Book #1)

August 2011

TRUTH

(Book #2)

October 2012

CONVICTED

(Book #3)

October 2013

REVEALED

(Book #4)

Previously titled: Behind His Eyes Convicted: The Missing Years

June 2014

BEYOND THE CONSEQUENCES

(Book #5)

January 2015

RIPPLES (Consequences stand-alone)

October 2017

CONSEQUENCES COMPANION READS:

BEHIND HIS EYES-CONSEQUENCES

January 2014

BEHIND HIS EYES-TRUTH

March 2014

* * *

STAND ALONE MAFIA THRILLER:

PRICE OF HONOR

Available Now

* * *

STAND-ALONE ROMANTIC THRILLER:

ON THE EDGE

May 2022

***

TALES FROM THE DARK SIDE SERIES:

INSIDIOUS

(All books in this series are stand-alone erotic thrillers)

Released October 2014

* * *

ALEATHA'S LIGHTER ONES:

PLUS ONE

Stand-alone fun, sexy romance

May 2017

ANOTHER ONE

Stand-alone fun, sexy romance

May 2018

ONE NIGHT

Stand-alone, sexy contemporary romance

September 2017

A SECRET ONE

April 2018

MY ALWAYS ONE

Stand-Alone, sexy friends to lovers contemporary romance

July 2021

QUINTESSENTIALLY THE ONE

Stand-alone, small-town, second-chance, secret baby contemporary romance

July 2022

ONE KISS

Stand-alone, small-town, best friend's sister, grump/sunshine contemporary romance.

July 2023

ONE STRING

Second-chance, enemies-to-lovers, fake-date, little-sister's-best-friend, forbidden, stand-alone contemporary romance

July 2024

INDULGENCE SERIES:

UNEXPECTED

August 2018

UNCONVENTIONAL

January 2018

UNFORGETTABLE

October 2019

UNDENIABLE

August 2020

ABOUT THE AUTHOR

Aleatha Romig is a New York Times, Wall Street Journal, and USA Today bestselling author who lives in Indiana, USA. She has raised three children with her high school sweetheart and husband of over thirty years. Before she became a full-time author, she worked days as a dental hygienist and spent her nights writing. Now, when she's not imagining mind-blowing twists and turns, she likes to spend her time with her family and friends. Her other pastimes include reading and creating heroes/anti-heroes who haunt your dreams!

Aleatha impresses with her versatility in writing. She released her first novel, CONSEQUENCES, in August of 2011. CONSEQUENCES, a dark romance, became a bestselling series with five novels and two companions released from 2011 through 2015. The compelling and epic story of Anthony and Claire Rawlings has graced more than half a million e-readers. Her first stand-alone smart, sexy thriller INSIDIOUS was next. Then Aleatha released the five-novel INFIDELITY series, a romantic suspense saga, that took the reading world by storm, the final book landing on three of the top bestseller lists. She ventured into traditional publishing with Thomas and Mercer. Her books INTO THE LIGHT and AWAY FROM THE DARK were published through this mystery/thriller publisher in 2016.

In the spring of 2017, Aleatha again ventured into a different genre with her first fun and sexy stand-alone romantic comedy with the USA Today bestseller PLUS ONE. She continued the “Ones” series with additional standalones, ONE NIGHT, ANOTHER ONE, MY ALWAYS ONE, and QUINTESSENTIALLY THE ONE. If you like fun, sexy, novellas that make your heart pound, try her “Indulgence series” with UNCONVENTIONAL. UNEXPECTED, UNFORGETTABLE, and UNDENIABLE.

In 2018 Aleatha returned to her dark romance roots with SPARROW WEBS. And continued with the mafia romance DEVIL'S DUET, and most recently her SINCLAIR DUET.

You may find all Aleatha's titles on her website.

Aleatha is a "Published Author's Network" member of the Romance Writers of America and PEN America. She is represented by SBR Media and Dani Sanchez with Wildfire Marketing.

facebook.com/aleatharomig
x.com/aleatharomig
instagram.com/aleatharomig

www.ingramcontent.com/pod-product-compliance
Lightning Source LLC
LaVergne TN
LVHW020701110826
845149LV00012B/2066

* 9 7 8 1 9 5 6 4 1 4 9 1 2 *